Catching the
Last Bus to Woodstock:
The Genesis of Inspector Morse

Ian Bradley

All correspondence for
Catching the Last Bus to Woodstock:
The Genesis of Inspector Morse
should be addressed to:

Irregular Special Press
Endeavour House
170 Woodland Road
Sawston
Cambridge
CB22 3DX

* ****

*****

This is a work of fiction. Names, characters, businesses, places,
events and incidents are either the products of the author's
imagination or used in a fictitious manner. Any resemblance to
actual persons, living or dead, or actual events is purely coincidental.

ISBN: 978 1 901091 81 6 (13 digit)

Cover Concept, Photographs & Editing: Antony J. Richards

Cover Illustration: A bus at its Woodstock terminus outside the Marlborough
Arms (see page 17), awaiting passengers for its return journey to Oxford.
Back Cover Illustration: The bus stop sign outside the
Marlborough Arms in Woodstock.
Bus icon by James Fenton from the Noun Project.

Contents

Colin Dexter OBE
(29th September 1930 – 21st March 2017)

Introduction

A journalist for one of the weekend supplements reviewing upon its publication in 1992 Colin Dexter's tenth Inspector Morse novel *The Way Through The Woods*, undertook some detective work of his own. He rang the number of The Bay Hotel, Lyme Regis listed on page 8 of the novel. Much to his surprise, someone answered the telephone. The number was genuine and the hotel actually existed.

The novel opens with Inspector Morse enjoying a holiday in Thomas Hardy country. Had the journalist delved a little more deeply, he would have discovered, upon Inspector Morse's return home to Oxford, that The Cotswold House bed and breakfast which features significantly later in the novel is also real. It stands on Banbury Road, Summertown still, some thirty years after it featured in *The Way Through The Woods*.

Rooting Inspector Morse in the real world of North Oxford and its environs was the particular genius of Colin Dexter and explains, in large part, the enduring appeal of the character he created. Dexter describes Oxford in forensic detail, rendering the characters of Inspector Morse, Sergeant Lewis, the denizens of 'town and gown' who inhabit this series of thirteen novels all the more memorable and immediate. In this particular novel, Dexter describes Morse traversing that territory which comprises the heart of the writer's world:

'At 5 p.m. (Morse) had walked down to Summertown and bought eight pint-cans of the newly-devised 'draught' bitter, which promised him the taste of a hand-pulled, cask-conditioned drop of ale; and two bottles of his favourite Quercy claret. For Morse – considerably out of condition still – the weight felt a bit too hefty; and outside the Radio Oxford building he halted a while and looked behind him in the hope of seeing the oblong outline of a red double-decker, coming up from the city centre. But there was no bus in sight, so he walked on. As (Morse) passed the Cotswold House he saw amongst other things the familiar white sign 'No Vacancies' on the door. He was not surprised. He had heard very well of the place. He wouldn't mind staying there himself. Especially for the breakfasts.'

5

[The Cotswold House bed and breakfast, which features significantly in the novel, is located in the Banbury Road close to Colin Dexter's home]

Morse's bachelor flat is situated in the fictional Leys Close, just off the real Banbury Road, two hundred yards from the Cotswold House and less than a minute's walk from the home of his creator who, since 1973, had lived in a modest semi- on the Banbury Road itself. Colin Dexter's place of work for 22 years was situated in Summertown, also. The University of Oxford Delegacy of Local Examinations for whom Dexter worked in his capacity of senior assistant secretary had their offices in Ewert House, some ten minutes' walk from his home.

In this age of the word processor, the computer with its winking cursor, its capacity to cut and paste, to delete, it is highly unlikely that a writer will complete an entire draft of their work in long hand. Writing his first novel between the years 1972 and 1974, and indeed for every subsequent novel in the Inspector Morse series, that is exactly how Colin Dexter worked, however. In an interview with *The Strand* magazine following publication of the final Morse novel in 1999, Dexter said:

'I wrote it in longhand, as I've done with all of my books. I've never typed a word of any book I've written. After I finished it, I went through from the beginning and crossed things out, like Dr. Johnson advised. "Whenever you've written anything particularly fine, strike it out!" When I was done, I rewrote it and got somebody to type it.'

That version of *Last Bus To Woodstock* completed on foolscap paper with blue ballpoint pen in Colin Dexter's neat, scholarly hand was stowed in the writer's loft for twenty-five years until it saw the light of day in 2000. It is this document which forms the basis of the present study.

As we shall see, most of the ingredients which made the Morse series such a success in both the novels and the television series were present in Dexter's first book. The text offers proof further of the ways in which Colin Dexter's stories are linked inextricably with, inspired even to a large extent by, the location in which Colin Dexter lived and worked.

Ian A Bradley

PRELUDE

~~Prelude~~

Femina pollex.

"Let's wait just a bit longer, please", said ~~Jennifer~~. "I'm
sure there's one due pretty soon."

~~But~~ She wasn't sure, and for the third time she turned to study
the time-table affixed in its rectangular frame to Fare stage 5.
But ~~Jennifer's~~ her mind had never journeyed with any confidence
in the world of columns and figures, and the finger tracing
its tentatively horizontal course from the left of the
~~time-table~~ frame had little chance of meeting, at the correct
co-ordinate, the finger descending in a vaguely vertical
line from the top. The girl standing beside her ~~moved~~ transferred her weight impatiently
from one foot to the other and said,
"I don' know abou' you." ~~said Sylvia~~.

"Just a minute. Just a minute". ~~Jennifer~~ she focussed yet
again on the ~~other~~ relevant columns : 4, 4A (not
after 18.00 hrs.), 4E, 4X (Saturdays only). Today
was Wednesday. That meant —. If 2 o'clock was
14.00 hours, that meant —.
"Look, ~~sweetheart~~, you please yourself bu' I'm going to hitch i'." Sylvia's habit of omitting all final 't's
~~seemed to Jennifer~~ ~~and seemed~~ irritatingly slack. 'It' in
Sylvia's diction was little more than the most
indeterminate of vowel sounds, articulated without the
slightest hint of a consonantal finale. If they
ever became better friends, ~~Jennifer~~ ~~would mention~~
~~it~~, ~~but she said nothing~~. it was something that ought to
be mentioned.
What time was it now? 6.45 p.m. That would be
18.45. Yes, she was getting ~~there~~ ~~somewhere at last~~.
"Come on. We'll ge' a lif' in no time, you see.
Tha's wha' half ~~these~~ ~~fellows~~ fellas are looking for —
a bi' o' skir'." ~~someone~~

Part One

Initium est dimidium facti
(The beginning is half of the deed)

Colin Dexter was often asked to recount the circumstances surrounding the creation of Inspector Morse. Dexter, his wife and their two children were holidaying in Wales, staying in a little guesthouse halfway between Caernarfon and Pwllheli. The writer recalled:

'It was often raining, and one Saturday afternoon when the rain was dribbling down the windows my children said to me, "Why don't you take us, like everybody else's father, to a place where the sun is shining and the sea is warm and you can catch crabs and get a suntan?" They said they wanted to go home so I said, "Well, you're not going home so just shut up and leave me alone." I shut myself into the kitchen and got a sheet of paper (I always wrote on lined paper) and started writing a story about a detective called Morse that very Saturday afternoon in August 1972. I don't suppose I wrote more than a page, or two or three paragraphs, but over the next eighteen months I kept on writing in spare moments. Obviously, I knew where it was going to be set – in Oxford – and I knew how it was going to end. I was always a whodunnit writer: my job is to entertain. I always wrote in longhand and got a dear old lady to type it out for me. I've never typed a word, never touched a computer key and never shall, but I can write quickly and legibly and so I was all right with a biro and ruled paper.'[1]

That page, those two or three paragraphs which Colin Dexter wrote on holiday, survives and it is therefore possible to trace the evolution of Dexter's first novel *Last Bus to Woodstock*, to discover the choices and changes he made to his manuscript as he wrote it, almost as if we are sitting beside him at the novel's creation.

---

[1] Interview with Theo Sloot, The Oxford Wine Company, *Stars in their bars.*

9

The first couple of pages of the novel comprise the Prelude. Dexter originally sub-titled his prologue *Femina pollex* which, loosely translated, means 'woman's thumb'. It is, then, an entirely appropriate tag line to a story which turns, essentially, on one young woman's attempt to hitch hike.

Like those crossword clues beloved of the book's author, though, these Latin tags often prove ambiguous. Pollex is derived from the Latin *pollere*: to be strong.

The phrase might also mean, therefore, 'strong women'. This is a theme on which not just this novel but also subsequent Morse books turn, particularly the final quartet. Like the sirens of Greek mythology, the particular kind of strength the women in the novels often exhibit is not what the male protagonists – Inspector Morse himself, chiefly, amongst them – take to be at face value. This is particularly true of this novel, a story about a man whose judgement, when push comes to shove, is found wanting. But then, like many of the recurring themes throughout the Morse novels, their DNA is contained within this first book.

Far from being the essentially passive, idealized figures of the male imagination, the woman in the novel often turns out to be the *primum mobile* and in this regard, the Morse novels are very closely related to the novels of American crime writer Raymond Chandler whose fictional alter ego Philip Marlowe inhabits a highly stylised world which, like Morse's, does not bear the scrutiny of a reviewer looking for psychological insight or social realism. That is not what the novels are about. They are operating on the level of myth or poetry, the only psychological insight the writer offers, his own.

Certainly, in this opening chapter, Sylvia proves headstrong, if nothing else, in securing a lift to The Black Prince public house but in so doing also seals her fate.

Her companion in this opening chapter is much less assertive in going about achieving her objectives:

"'Let's wait just a bit longer, please," are the first words of the novel.'

In the published version, these words are spoken by 'the girl in dark-blue trousers and the light summer coat'. In his manuscript, however, Colin Dexter referred to her as Jennifer. It is not clear at what point Dexter decided not to name the girl in the opening pages of the novel. The reason why he decided she should remain anonymous is obvious: to let her name be unknown at this point increases the mystery. As Morse begins his investigation, not only the detective but the reader as well must try to discover the identity of the other girl at the bus stop that fateful night.

More significantly for the evolution of the novel itself, however, it transpires that whilst a character in the novel is subsequently given the name Jennifer, this is not the girl who was at the bus stop. Dexter, therefore, creates yet another suspect who comes within the orbit of the sordid events surrounding Sylvia's death. And he may have decided that this anonymous girl at the bus stop should assume a much greater importance for both the novel and Morse himself than the girl who is later called Jennifer.

Colin Dexter therefore systematically rules through Jennifer's name each time it is used in the opening pages of the novel, either substituting pronouns or rendering the action of the verb in the passive tense. At the crucial moment in the Prelude, Dexter substitutes the word 'Sweetheart' for 'Jenny':

> "'Look, sweetheart, you please yourself bu' I'm going to hitch.'"

This is the defining moment of the novel, bringing to a close a beautifully sketched moment where the mystery girl struggles to make sense of the bus timetable. She may or may not be more intelligent than Sylvia. Perhaps Sylvia would have understood the timetable much more easily than her more conventional friend but she lacks the patience to wait. The girl's irritation with Sylvia's 'slack' way of speaking – omitting all final t's – is fed by her frustration at being unable to comprehend the timetable. She is much more tolerant towards Sylvia when she realizes that eighteen forty-five hours equates to quarter to seven in the evening: 'Yes, she was getting somewhere at last.'

Sylvia's numerous interruptions only serve to prevent her friend from working out the vagaries of the timetable. Colin Dexter describes the process with forensic attention to detail. Research is clearly in evidence and there can be no doubt that anyone perusing a history of public transport in Oxford in the 1970s could be assured that the route between Oxford and Woodstock was run by buses designated '4, 4A (not after 18.00 hours), 4E, 4X (Saturdays only)'.

The girl's sense of social superiority to Sylvia reaches its apotheosis in a remark in the original manuscript which Colin Dexter excised for the published version:

> 'Yes, your sort will always be all right she thought.'

It is unclear why this comment was cut. Perhaps its evident snobbery would alienate the reader's sympathies for the girl. It was a direct response to Sylvia's 'We'll be all righ'' but on what basis was the girl making such a judgement? True, in Sylvia's diction 'It' was 'little more than the most indeterminate of vowel sounds, articulated without the slightest hint of a consonantal finale' but this is slender evidence for such a sweeping condemnation. Perhaps it was the giggle they would be "'avin'" in the morning which prompted such defensiveness.

There is no doubt that despite the fact there may be little to choose between the two girls' cognitive abilities, the mysterious friend, at least, in this scene shows some capacity for logical thought and reflection, as her resolution that Sylvia should be challenged about her casual diction should they 'ever become better friends'.

Sylvia shows no such sign of the ability to reflect. She works from some sort of intuition seated in the emotional or the physical which craves immediate gratification. The two girls are a classic representation of the dislocation between the literate and the merely literal, the satisfying of Sylvia's needs being the engine of the story, the friction of the fiction which actually moves the plot forward, whilst her companion can offer only commentary. The relationship between the educated and uneducated classes, perhaps, 'town and gown', was ever thus.

The contrast is never more evident than in the fact that whilst her friend wrestles with the temporal – 'What time was it now? 6.45 pm. That would be 18.45. Yes, she was getting somewhere (in the original manuscript, 'there') at last' – Sylvia embraces the merely carnal in order to reach her destination:

'Come on. We'll ge' a lif' in no time, you see. Tha's wha' half these fellas are looking for – a bi' o' skir'.'

Originally Colin Dexter had written '...in truth, Jennifer had no reason whatsoever to question Sylvia's brisk optimism' which was amended to '... in truth, there appeared no reason whatsoever ...' the writer, once again, masking the identity of Sylvia's friend.

The novel, as published, reads 'No accommodating motorist could fail to be impressed by her minimal skirting and the lovely invitation of the legs below.'

Colin Dexter's first choice of word, however, for the response of the interested driver was 'tempted'. There may be two reasons why this was changed: first, there may well be drivers who were not tempted by the minimal skirting and, second, if that is the reason behind Sylvia's demise, the word does rather anticipate the turn the story may be about to take. Wisely, Colin Dexter decides not to anticipate these dreadful events although the reader may well be ahead of him.

And so, Colin Dexter writes in the original manuscript, 'holding one gloved hand to the collar of her lightweight summer coat, she ran with awkward splay-footed gait in pursuit of her Sylvia, *femina pollex*, the professional hitch-hiker.'

Who is this mysterious girl who accompanied Sylvia on her last journey? What happened to her? Why did she not come forward when the death of Sylvia was made known to the public? Just as much as the reasons for the death of Sylvia, solving the identity of her friend becomes an essential part of the mystery to the extent that Part One of the novel is entitled *Search for a Girl* which in turn is virtually a leitmotif for the Morse series.

Of course, without a witness to her presence at the bus stop, the reader would be in possession of a clue which is denied to the officers investigating the crime. It is necessary, therefore, that a witness is produced who saw this second girl and so Colin Dexter introduces the character of Mrs. Jarman.

Over the space of just a couple of pages, the writer sketches deftly the outline of Mrs. Jarman's lonely life, the writer taking great pains in the manuscript to excise the phrase 'so many of her friends' from her reflections on the quality of television programmes for a more passive construction, 'She could never understand why there was so much criticism of the programmes,' to emphasize her isolation.

And, indeed, it seems Mrs. Jarman's life itself is a somewhat passive construction. Perhaps the most telling phrase Colin Dexter used about her was the way he describes her semi-detached house. The phrase which appears in the novel is 'pride-and-poverty' but the words which were used originally were 'quietly modest.'

It would be difficult to apply this epithet to Sylvia's demeanour and behaviour which is anything but, the life Mrs. Jarman, has chosen for herself shown in sharp relief to such exhibitionism. Nevertheless, she is implicated in Sylvia's fate, however, if for no other reason than the reply she gives to the mystery girl's enquiry about the next bus ('it's just for Yarnton. It goes to the village, then turns round and comes back') leads both girls to conclude that they have missed the last bus to Woodstock and that they might as well go for broke, therefore, by hitching a lift.

When the next bus does arrive following the girls' departure on foot, and it transpires the vehicle is indeed destined for Woodstock, Mrs. Jarman consoles herself with the belief that 'They would either get a lift or see the bus and manage to get to the next stop' is, sadly, wide of the mark. The interjection of the enquiring

13

officer at this point in the novel: 'How long had they been gone, Mrs. Jarman?' serves almost as a Greek chorus. Sylvia will have been gone for a very long time: Mrs. Jarman's condition at half past ten – 'sound asleep' – standing in stark contrast to Sylvia's own: 'brutally murdered'.

Part Two

The Mystery of the Black Prince

We have explored the circumstances which drove Colin Dexter to begin work on his first novel and studied the creation of those first couple of pages he wrote on holiday in Wales. What was the inspiration for the plot, however? The clue to this is in the pages of the novel itself. It is a story Colin Dexter himself told many times when giving talks at his book signing sessions and he wove the anecdote into the pages of *Last Bus to Woodstock*.

In chapter 16 of the novel, Sergeant Lewis is driving from the city centre to police headquarters at Kidlington. *En route*, he spies a hitchhiker with long, blonde hair who is 'sticking out a hopeful thumb'. Lewis is surprised to discover as the car draws past that the hitchhiker is, in fact, a male with beard and side-whiskers. This incident actually happened to Colin Dexter and the autobiographical link between the writer and his chief protagonist is evident in the fact that Dexter originally writes the name of the driver as 'mo– … Morse …'

'Let's hope nothing happens to this one, he thought', Dexter writes originally, although the rueful reflection of Sergeant Lewis is subsequently excised.

In the novel, this brief encounter occurs outside the large engineering block which stands on 'the right fork' of 'the broad tree-lined sweep of St Giles'.

It is at this junction that the description begins of the route from Oxford to Woodstock with which Chapter One of the novel opens.

But then, a sense of real place is essential to the series of Inspector Morse novels and never more so than on Morse's home turf, the city of Oxford.

Absolute fidelity to topographical detail creates the sense that these are events unfolding like a gazetteer of a real time and a real place, delineating the lives of people as real as the ale Chief Inspector Morse is wont to imbibe.

[St. Giles' looking toward the War Memorial where the road splits into the Woodstock Road (left) and Banbury Road (right)]

The description is couched in prose which would be worthy of a tourist's guidebook or travelogue. Initially, Colin Dexter's description concerns itself only with the route taken by the twin Banbury and Woodstock Roads but, as the description develops, he takes a brief detour, inserted after the first sentence, to deal with Oxford's preoccupation with traffic which was present thirty years ago when the novel first appeared and continues to exercise the municipal city forefathers:

'... each must first cross the bust northern ring road, along which streams of frenetic motorists speed by, gladly avoiding (in the manuscript, 'eschewing') the delights of the old university city.'

The destination for the journey Colin Dexter delineates is that of the two girls at the bus stop: The Black Prince.

In the novel as published, Dexter situates The Black Prince 'half-way down a broad-side-street to the left as one is journeying north.' In the original manuscript, the novelist is still in travelogue mode, writing:

'The motorist who takes the first turning left off the main street will find (an embarrassing) himself ...'

The phrase 'an embarrassing' is scored through twice so quite what the motorist will find which is so embarrassing, we will never know.

The public house upon which Colin Dexter based The Black Prince, in the car park of which Sylvia Kaye met such a grisly end has been variously identified as being based on The Bear which is situated on Park Street in Woodstock or The Marlborough Arms on Oxford Street. There is, presently, a public house called The Black Prince in Woodstock. This is situated at some distance from the location Colin Dexter describes in the novel and is on the A44, heading out of Woodstock towards Evesham. There was no public house with this name when the novel was first published. It is very prescient, therefore, for Colin Dexter, describing the origins of 'his' Black Prince to write:

'Truth to tell, a director of the London company which bought the old house, stable-yards and all, some ten (in the manuscript, five) years since, had noticed in some dubiously authenticated guidebook, that somewhere thereabouts the prince was born. The director had been warmly congratulated by his Board for this felicitous piece of research, and not less for his subsequent discovery that the noble Prince did not as yet figure in the Woodstock telephone directory.'

Colin Dexter's own fictional pub then 'can claim no ancient pedigree'. The real Black Prince public house must, therefore, have similarly shallow roots in the

17

town. This seems to be borne out by the pub's management who believe the hostelry, which was formerly known as The Wheatsheaf, was re-named The Black Prince in 1984, some nine years after *Last Bus to Woodstock* was first published. Whether the appearance of the fictional Black Prince pub had any bearing on the re-naming of the actual public house is a matter of speculation for local historians.

[The Bear (top left and right) is certainly situated 'half-way down a broad-side-street to the left as one is journeying north' but is a hotel (bottom left) and not close to a bus stop. It is similar in appearance to The Marlborough Arms (bottom right) which is situated on the main road through Woodstock. Both have arches which originally led to car parks]

What is beyond doubt, however, is that this is an excellent name for the pub in the courtyard of which Sylvia Kaye's body was found, the adjective bringing with it, as it does, associations of death. Indeed, before he could ascend the throne,

Edward died in 1376 at the age of forty-five years old, coincidentally Colin Dexter's age when the novel was first published. Edward was given the soubriquet 'black', it is believed, after his death, partly because of the colour of his armour and partly because of the significant military successes he gained against the French at the Battle of Crecy in 1346.

Colin Dexter's account of the manager's attempts to legitimize the Black Prince's association with his hostelry is elaborated upon quite comically. The source of his 'gifted' daughter's transcription of the details of Edward's birth is a later addition, in green ink, to the manuscript – 'a children's encyclopedia' – which adds to the infantile attempt at deception. The browning of the 'manuscript' in the oven, equally, is characteristic of the wearisome sort of assignment the girl might be set at school in History. This is only one more example of the deceit which runs through the novel. Whilst Colin Dexter argues that 'it seems highly improbable, alas, that the warrior son of King Edward III had ever laughed or cried or tippled or wenched in any of its precincts' and is, therefore, to all intents and purposes, aside from being dead for nearly six hundred years, not a suspect in the case, nevertheless it is the suspicion that these sorts of activities – particularly 'wenching' – have been committed within the precincts of the pub, and specifically the courtyard that forms the basis of the present investigation.

We are introduced to Gaye, the 'hostess' of the Black Prince, a euphemism bestowed upon her by the same manager who fabricated such a dubious lineage for the pub. The sentiments behind his elevation of her title from the more lugubrious 'barmaid' are entirely shared by Gaye. Colin Dexter originally wrote: 'Seldom was she called upon to deal with such a proletarian request as "A pint o' your best bitter, luv!"'

But this snobbery is made Gaye's own and rendered even more pointedly in the version contained in the published novel:

'"A pint of your best bitter, luv," was a request Gaye seldom had to meet and she now associated it with the proletariat.'

Despite her own chequered past, the woman eschews sentimentality (potential suitors to her divorced status are 'mawkish', a later addition to the manuscript) to the point of intolerance of others' weaknesses, although this is, largely, excised from the final version of the novel.

Called 'Brenda' at one point in the manuscript (perhaps Dexter's original name for the character), a divorced woman with 'two young children', she is very dismissive of the drunken young man who is later to discover Sylvia's body and be the first witness in the police investigation.

When the young man says 'Same again', she looks at him not 'quizzically' as the published version of the novel has it but 'critically.'

'I don't think you can take much more was only the thought in Brenda's critical glance' Dexter wrote originally.

Giving 'Brenda' one son rather than two children may have softened the character, however, and allowed her imaginative sympathies to extend rather more effectively to the drunken young man sitting at the bar asking for a whisky when she calls 'last orders'.

'She knew he would soon be sick' Colin Dexter wrote originally but this premonition is excised from the version sent for typing. Dexter similarly expunges the lugubrious phrase 'on this fateful evening' as the young man stumbles his way to the further reaches of the dark, cobbled courtyard, the far corner of which in the original manuscript is 'fit for the guilty purposes of night.' These phrases, which would not look out of place in a soliloquy from Lady Macbeth, now cut, allow the full horror of what the young man is about to discover to arrive unheralded. The reader, however, is prepared for the revelation because Chapter One returns us neatly to that same point in time we had reached at the end of the Prelude.

Part Three

Chief Inspector Morse

The original title for Chapter 2 of *Last Bust to Woodstock* was *Chief Inspector Morse* as it sees the introduction of the eponymous detective to the world.

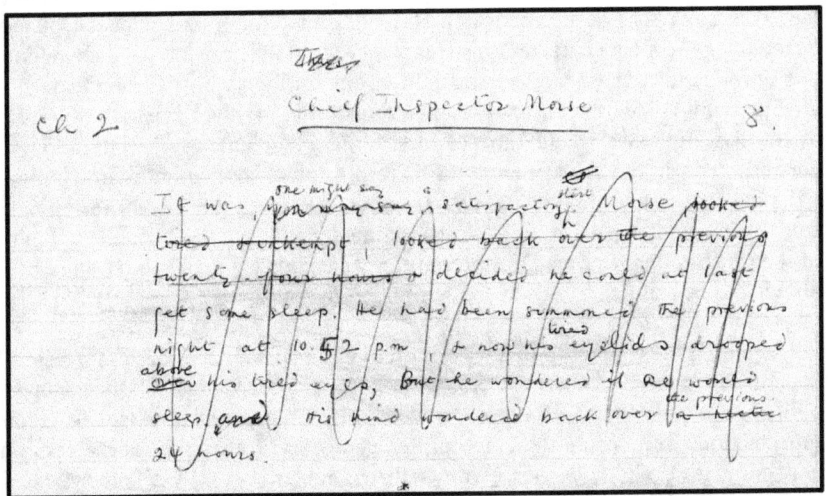

In the published version of the novel, the chapters carry only the dates on which the events described took place: *Wednesday, 29 September*. It can be no coincidence that Inspector Morse's first appearance in print occurs on the same date as his creator's birthday.

Like his final appearance, Morse's debut very nearly takes place in bed. The very first words Colin Dexter wrote about Chief Inspector Morse in the manuscript have been subsequently expunged and have not appeared in print until now.

Chapter 2 begins:

'It was, you might say, a satisfactory start. Morse looked tired and unkempt,'

Dexter amends 'you might say' to 'one might say' and the disheveled state of Morse is excised completely. The paragraph then reads:

'It was, one might say, a satisfactory start. Morse looked back over the previous twenty-four hours and decided he could at last get some sleep. He had been summoned the previous night at 10.52 (amended from 10.42), and now his tired eyelids drooped above (initially, 'over') his tired eyes, but he wondered if he would sleep and his mind wondered (sic) back over the previous (originally 'a hectic') 24 hours.'

This paragraph is then struck through with a line of green ink like a waveform. Whether Colin Dexter intended to relate the previous twenty-four hours of the case in 'flashback' with Morse recalling the progress of the case to date, we cannot tell. It is clear that he decided as a strategy either for framing the chapter or introducing the main character, this was a very unsatisfactory start and abandoned this introduction. There may be several reasons for this: whilst Colin Dexter has already manipulated the chronology of events, bringing the reader 'the future in the instant' in the way he juxtaposes Mrs. Jarman's thoughts at the bus stop with her responses in the subsequent, and therefore future, police interview, he may have felt that to narrate a whole chapter after the fact might distance the reader from events and jeopardize that forensic immediacy which has been the hallmark of the prose so far. The reader may well feel cheated, as though she has not been allowed to be privy to events as they unfolded in real time.

Beginning the chapter in this way, moreover, makes much more of an issue of the introduction of Chief Inspector Morse. In the chapter as it appears in the published novel, Morse's entrance must rank amongst the most inauspicious introductions for a major character in literary history. It is typical of the restraint and good taste Colin Dexter exhibits throughout the novels where Morse is concerned, helping to feed that sense that Morse is, ultimately, and remains something of a mystery himself.

His arrival in this first novel – in the second of two police cars – is unheralded bar a small knot of onlookers and his name is introduced almost casually a good page and a half into the chapter:

'There were over fifty people to see, and Morse realized that it would take some time.'

The first historic meeting on the page between Morse and Lewis is equally understated. We learn the Sergeant's name before that of the Chief Inspector and that, prior to the events described in this novel, the two men were, perhaps, on nodding terms:

'He knew Sergeant Lewis only slightly, but soon found himself pleasurably impressed by the man's level-headed competence.'

This sentence is hard won, however, Colin Dexter taking as much trouble to revise their first meeting as he does the introduction of his detective. The arrival of Chief Inspector Morse and his first encounter with Sergeant Lewis is written somewhat differently in the manuscript, scored through, as the opening paragraph of the novel had been, and re-drafted on a leaf which is then interposed in the manuscript.

The original scene was written as follows:

'Five minutes later a second police car arrived, and all eyes turned to the man for whom ... who got out of the back.'

This phrase is then excised and Dexter continues:

'... turned to the lightly-built dark (-haired) man who alighted. He conferred ...'

It was amended to 'conversed very briefly with Sergeant Lewis ...' Here, then is their very first conversation but Dexter scores through the Sergeant's name and substitutes '... the constable who stood guard outside' thus deferring their first meeting hereafter. The paragraph continues:

'... nodded his head approvingly several times and walked into the Black Prince.'

There then follows a paragraph which is scored through completely and which does not make the published version of the novel:

'S. Lewis appeared to be doing all the right things and Morse left him to supervise the routine tasks. Each customer ... and everyone on the premises was asked ... All were being asked to give names and addresses of all persons on the premises were taken and a brief statement of their evening's whereabouts, car registrations and destinations.'

Morse's first glimpse of the body is also described in a substantially different way in Dexter's first draft. He writes:

'From a side entrance, Morse himself (and this is the very first time Morse's name would appear in this version) stepped gingerly out into the courtyard and shone his torch around, and walked slowly to the sprawling figure of the young girl. She lay face downwards on her left side, her long blond hair cruelly streaked with matted blood. He trod carefully and shone his torch (carefully) around the ground and walked slowly up to the girl. It was clear that she had been killed by a heavy blow across the back of the skull –probably from the position of the body – a bloodstained stick, flat heavy spanner about $1\frac{1}{2}$ inches in diameter across and about 2 feet long, lay by the far wall. (For a few minutes), he stood motionless for a few minutes gazing down at the ugly scene at his feet.'

A conversation on the whereabouts of some arc lamps, specified as eight in the manuscript, follows directly, the constable concluding, in response to Morse's contention that they needed some arc lamps. 'Yes, I suppose so'. This is amended in the published version to:

    '"It would help, I suppose, sir."
    "Get some."
    "Me, sir?"
    "Yes, you!"
    "Where shall I get …?"
    "How the hell do I know," bellowed Morse.'

In all probability, Colin Dexter, the Poet Laureate of the police procedural over the course of the Morse novels, doesn't know either, Morse's ire on this point, therefore, introducing some comedy into the otherwise grim scene. In the manuscript Colin Dexter writes:

    'It took an hour before the lamps were ready'

But this information doesn't make the published version, although if the time Morse first received the call in the original opening to the chapter – approximately ten to eleven – stands, then, by implication, an hour has indeed passed before Lewis completes his task of interviewing the witnesses at a quarter to midnight.

In the excised paragraph with the comment that 'S. Lewis appeared to be doing all the right things', the reader is being asked to imagine that Lewis is himself conducting those interviews at that moment. By assigning a second constable prior to the interviews, Morse, and by implication, therefore, clearly Colin Dexter himself, is both conferring more respect on the sergeant (Dexter does write in the published version of this scene that Morse 'found himself pleasurably impressed by the man's level-headed competence') and deferring the first meeting proper between Morse and Lewis to a time when it can be given more attention: the partnership between the two colleagues clearly central to Dexter's conception from the outset.

If Lewis is engaged in this way, this also gives Morse – and Dexter – more time to pay full attention to the crime in the courtyard. The original description was curtailed, perhaps because Dexter knew he wanted to re-work the whole page in its entirety and much more description is written on the new, interposed leaf of the manuscript, 11a.

The phrase 'probably from the position of the body' is discarded; the hypothesis Morse is about to build from his first sight of the dead girl not pursued. In the original version, the murder weapon is described as 'a bloodstained stick about 1 ½ inches in diameter across and about 2 feet long'.

In the published novel, this is changed to the actual blunt instrument which was used to effect the crime, 'a flat heavy tyre-spanner' and Dexter expends quite a lot of additional detail in the final version, describing the implement. Matters of motoring feature quite heavily in the revised, final version of this passage and although Colin Dexter's novels are, generally, timeless, one particular observation does date the book to headier and more carefree days:

'... (Morse) wondered by what feats of advanced-motoring skill and precision their inebriated owners could ever negotiate the vehicles unscathed through the narrow exit from the yard.'

It is quite unusual that a senior member of the constabulary should reflect on the risks drivers who drink run in scratching the paintwork of their cars rather than the risks they run in injuring, or killing, themselves or other road users. But of course, in making this observation, Dexter is actually leaving another clue for the reader with regard to the circumstances surrounding Sylvia's demise.

Unlike her companion at the bus stop, who was wearing 'a light summer coat', Sylvia was dressed only in 'a very brief, dark-blue mini-skirt and a white blouse. Nothing else.' Truly, there was the risk that she might catch her death.

'The left-hand side of the blouse was ripped across; the top two buttons were unfastened and the third had been wrenched away, leaving the full breasts almost totally exposed.'

The salacious mood extends even to the discovery of a mother-of-pearl button which has been torn loose from the blouse and which Morse finds near the body which seems to be 'winking' at the detective, as though offering some sort of collusion. Morse's attitude to all this is made quite evident, however, in the sentiment expressed: 'How he hated sex murders!' In the manuscript, this is made even stronger when Dexter writes 'but now he suspected ... feared the worst'. Quite what that 'worst' might be, we shall never be privy to for Dexter excises the statement and does not develop the point.

25

It is unlikely that such speculation and the viewing of the body took Morse the hour Lewis and the second constable spent interviewing witnesses. There is more sly humour here, then, when an undisclosed part of that hour must have been spent by Morse in the manager's office drinking 'what looked very much like neat' whisky which is what Morse is doing when Lewis reports to him.

The following scene establishes quite brilliantly Morse's preoccupations, his parsimonious attitude towards his colleague and the nature of their forthcoming partnership. Their exchange also contains the biggest clue, certainly, to Morse's progress throughout the novel but which escapes the attention of even the great detective.

'"Ah Lewis." He thrust the paper across. "Have a look at 14 down. Appropriate eh?" Sergeant Lewis looked down at the clue 14 down: *Take in Bachelor? It could do (3)*. He saw what Morse had written in to the completed diagram: BRA.' What was he supposed to say? He had never worked with Morse before.'

Morse's explanation of the clue is explained a little more pompously in the manuscript:

'"Bachelor is BA," said Morse "& take denotes the letter 'r'; recipe in Latin. Did you never do any Latin, Sergeant?"'

Morse considers this to be a 'Good clue, don't you think?' but it proves to be an even better and more appropriate clue than the Chief Inspector could possibly imagine: for in *Last Bus to Woodstock*, the bachelor who is taken in most completely is Morse himself. Placing such a clue at this point in the story only demonstrates the author's brio; how completely he is master of his novel and with what guile and humour he is playing with his readers.

Lewis' response to Morse's suggestion that he might be wasting the sergeant's time ('Yes, sir') only confirms Morse's belief that Lewis is 'a man of some honesty and integrity', again establishing the nature of their relationship over the course of the thirteen novels and numerous short stories. Like a Classics master prompting a favoured pupil, Morse elicits the spirited and independent response he wants and their relationship is confirmed.

With his demonstrable sense of humour, Colin Dexter undercuts the whole scene, however, and again sets a precedent for the two police officers' relationship when Morse denies Lewis the whisky he has himself just ordered when he tells the landlord 'Sergeant Lewis is on duty ...'

Double whisky and double standards ...

Interestingly, in the manuscript, Morse refers to the landlord not as Mr. Westbrook of the published novel but Mr. Kaye, the surname Dexter would eventually assign to the murdered girl, her full name being conspicuous by its absence in the opening chapter and to date. Bates is another name Dexter considers before settling for Westbrook.

Dexter adds an extra sentence which was excised in the manuscript and never appeared in print:

'The manager hastened away and Lewis was not the only one to feel puzzled.'

The partnership of Morse and Lewis is, however, indeed a cause for celebration and with only a few deft strokes, Colin Dexter here sketches in the dynamic of their relationship for the rest of the series. In considering the Chief Inspector's offer, Lewis looks straight into Morse's eyes and finds himself saying he would be 'delighted'.

It is the quality of Morse's eyes which seems often to have an effect on a first encounter. Colin Dexter goes to some trouble to get the description just right. Initially, Morse's eyes are described as 'piercing' grey and then 'steely' before he settles on 'hard'. An entire sentence, unfortunately, fails to make the final draft where Lewis feels that the Inspector's eyes 'seemed to look straight into his mind'. Clearly, Morse's stare is compelling, not to say arresting. This is certainly found to be so by the barmaid, Gaye whose eyes 'met and held his briefly as he came in entered, & there was she felt a strange strong compulsion about (this) the man. It was not as if so much that he were seemed mentally (to be) undressing her, as most (of the) men she knew, it was but as if she he had already had (done so). She looked at listened to him with interest as he spoke.'

Their brief and ultimately fruitless flirtation here sets the pattern for the larger novel and indeed Morse's career as a whole, the barmaid concluding, reluctantly, that the exchange they share is sadly nowhere near as satisfying as it seems to be in books: 'It wasn't exactly what she'd come to expect from her reading of Holmes or Poirot ...'

What leaves her dissatisfied, specifically on this occasion, is the Chief Inspector's address to the waiting witnesses in the restaurant. This section initially gave Colin Dexter some trouble. In gathering the suspects together to be addressed by his great detective, Dexter wrote originally:

'(When all had gathered In the restaurant, it was at 12.15 am)

At 12.15 am on the morning of 30 September, Morse addressed the gathered throng in the restaurant, where there was ample space for the/everyone ...'

Whilst Morse's address to the assembly is given as reported speech in the published version of the novel, in draft, Dexter originally conceived of the speech as being given by Morse directly. Morse says:

'Ladies and gentlemen ... I want to thank you for your co-operation. I know you have been inconvenienced for this I am sorry about this. You know why I am here – there has been a murder. A young girl lies in the courtyard – murdered. I don't yet know who she is but she's a blonde. Since we don't know yet who the murdered girl is, all cars in the courtyard must naturally stay there until tomorrow; Sergeant Lewis here has already rung for a fleet of taxis; a few are already here. If anyone here wishes to report to me or to Sergeant Lewis anything whatsoever at all which may be of interest or value – however trivial unimportant it may seem to you – I must ask such a person to stay behind now. The rest of you may go.'

For Gaye McFee, 'the little speech seemed ... rather an uninspired performance.' In one sentence which does not make the published version, the bar maid, tellingly, reflects:

'What had he said? "I don't know who she is".'

In an effort to make her life a little less prosaic, the barmaid does attempt to volunteer some information in order to move things forward but becomes merely embroiled in a rather ill-tempered exchange with the Chief Inspector. Initially, Morse's curiosity is piqued at what she has to tell him:

'That's most very interesting, Miss er Miss er – or is it er?'

Significantly, Gaye replies, initially, in the manuscript 'Mrs. Jarman' which is, of course, the name of the witness at the bus stop in the Prelude. Possibly this was a simple error on Colin Dexter's part or, like the other names – Jennifer, Brenda – the novelist has not yet fixed the characters' names entirely.

'"Mrs. Mrs McFee"
"I thought you might have been wearing those rings to frighten off the randy brigade who must come to drool over you, Mrs. Jarman."'

Morse's language is rather more moderated in the published version and tempered by the addition of the phrase 'Please forgive me, Mrs. McFee.' The barmaid's reaction remains the same, however:

'Gaye felt very angry.'

Colin Dexter super scribes in green ink just the phrase 'Hateful man', refining it to 'He was a hateful man.'

Significantly, Dexter also changes the line 'Look, inspector or whoever you are' to 'Look, inspector whatever your name is'. The world was not to learn his Christian name, at any rate, for another twenty-one years.

Morse quite clearly hits a nerve here, the reader having already learned in Chapter Two that 'A flash of gems on the second and third fingers of (Gaye's) left hand, betokened gentle warning to the mawkish amateur playboy, and perhaps – as some maintained – a calculated invitation to the wealthy professional philanderer.'

It is difficult to judge whether Morse's overtures are predatory, conciliatory or a mixture of both:

'Mrs. Jarman (sic),' broke in Morse gently, looking at her with gentle weariness an open nakedness in his eyes, 'If I lived anywhere near, I'd come in myself and drool over you every night of the week.'

We may find in favour of conciliatory then on this point, particularly since Dexter used the phrase 'gentle weariness' originally rather than the more lugubrious 'open nakedness'.

The effects his words have on the barmaid, moreover, clearly mollify her in a sentence which the writer (perhaps denying himself any sort of sentimentality in this earliest incarnation of Morse) excises from the published version:

'And Gaye with a sudden inexplicable hurt deep down inside her, suddenly wished that he did live somewhere near.'

Or the writer's alternative line:

'And Gaye with a sudden inexplicable hurt deep down inside her, was unable to decide whether she herself wished it so or not.'

Such a tender conclusion to their brief exchange is not in prospect when the bar maid first approaches Morse with her information. Initially 'Morse looked at her, held her eyes with naked … and slowly nodded.'

Colin Dexter was clearly determined to work the adjective 'naked' into his description of Morse's glance at some point and the initial attraction is clearly in evidence.

Gaye's own evidence is originally written as: 'I saw the young fellow who found her with a girl like that last week'.

Perhaps because the rhythm of the sentence is something more akin to the opening line of a music hall song and the emphasis is on the man who discovered the victim rather than the victim herself, Colin Dexter amends the sentence in the final version to:

"'I think she was here last week – she was with the man who found her body tonight. I saw them here. I work in the lounge.'"

'There was, of course, the young man who had found the girl ... She had seen him before, but she couldn't quite remember who it was he'd been with, or when. And then – she suddenly remembered – she had it – blonde hair! She'd been in the lounge with him only last – yes – last week. But then But a lot of girls these days had blonde peroxided their hair.'

The word 'peroxided' is super scribed on the manuscript in blue ink. It is a significant addition and worth reflecting on. Although the word is not used, nor – one assumes meant – pejoratively it is an interesting assumption on the auburn-haired barmaid's part. The discrepancy between what 'seems' and what 'is' forms a vital part of the crime writer's armoury and, like Shakespeare, in this and many of the subsequent novels in the Morse series, Colin Dexter is often preoccupied with the ramifications of the word. It is not the young man himself Gaye remembers but the blonde hair of his companion. The barmaid's motive in bringing this to Morse's attention is unclear, beyond, perhaps, trying to bring some romance and excitement into her life. However construed, her intervention only makes matters worse for the young man: for, either he was on more than nodding acquaintance with the murder victim, having been with her in the same pub only the week before or he is in the habit of squiring young women (preferably blonde) to public houses.

An equally pressing question is why the young man was drinking so heavily on the night Sylvia was murdered. Either Gaye is not given the opportunity to tell the policemen about the man's inebriated state or Colin Dexter chooses not to recount this episode. In any case, Morse is able to work something out for himself about the young man's state from a closer examination of the courtyard which takes place prior to Inspector Morse's first published interview with his first suspect.

The arc lamps, which were such a bone of contention for Morse when he arrived on the scene, have now been fixed in relay around the perimeter of the yard. Colin Dexter excises the line 'After hearing the significant information forwarded volunteered by Mrs. Gaye McFee, Morse had instructed Lewis to ~~hold~~ detain the unfortunate ~~lad~~ young man ...'

Either Colin Dexter felt that what Mrs. McFee had volunteered was not, in the great scheme of things, so significant or he simply wanted to emphasise Morse's ability to find clues by other means than witness statements.

An interesting exchange then takes place between the detectives which sheds much light on the differing priorities of the two men, particularly in the more detailed version in the manuscript.

Dexter wrote originally:

'As Sergeant Lewis looked down on her, he felt a little sad for all his policeman's training ...'
This then amended to:

'something of the tears of things'

And then:

'a deep sadness in his soul'

Before the final published version which yields a much more professional and objective response, perhaps:

'deep revulsion against the violence and senselessness of murder'

In contrast, Morse has his sights fixed on higher things:

'"Do you study the stars, Lewis?" he asked
"I read the horoscopes sometimes, sir."
"No, no, I mean the constellations."'

Dexter expunges Morse's clarification on the point of astronomy, choosing to have Lewis's misapprehension fall on deaf ears. Morse then proceeds to recount a story about a group of schoolchildren who set themselves to collect a million matches.

The nonplussed response of Lewis to this anecdote is recorded in the published novel as simply: 'Lewis thought it his duty to say something, but all appropriate comment eluded him'.

This is a deftly comic touch. What would a comment appropriate to the circumstances be? Something about haystacks and needles, perhaps? Some reference to the Herculean nature of the task the night's events had brought them?

31

The connection between Morse's astral preoccupations and the anecdote about the matches is not made here although it was in Dexter's original version which reads:

> 'Lewis thought it his duty to follow the Inspector's heavenly gaze.
> "What's he want me to say?" thought Lewis.
> "Don't you think, Lewis, they could have saved a lot of time, if they really wanted to get some concept of number a really big number, by looking at all these stars out there?"
> "I'm not sure I know what 'concept' means", said Lewis
> "Do you know," said Morse, "That's the most intelligent statement I've heard tonight."'

It is understandable why the writer made the excisions he did at this point, although it is fascinating to see Dexter testing and rejecting the dynamic between his two officers – Holmes and Watson – reigning in some of the more excessive elements of the comedy so that Lewis does not become an obtuse Dr. Watson of Nigel Bruce-like proportions.

Dexter wrote originally:

> 'After what seemed to Lewis a long time a while, Morse reverted his gaze from the celestial city to the to more terrestrial objects things and the two of them looked down again at the murdered girl.'

Whilst we lose the perspective from the phrases 'what seemed to Lewis a long time' and 'the celestial city' with its striking contrast to the darkened car park, Dexter retains an element of that juxtaposition – almost cinematic in the scope of its sweep – by adding in blue ballpoint pen:

> 'The spanner and the solitary white button lay where Morse had seen them earlier. There was nothing else.'

This is not enough for the writer, however, and he seeks a more powerful way to conclude this section. Having lost the reflection on 'the celestial city', with its attendant shift in perspective, Dexter adds an intensifier to his final sentence:

> 'There was nothing much else'

And then, in green ink appends the final graphic detail:

> '... to see but for the trail of (dried) blood that led almost from one end of the back wall to the other'.

Part Four

Now she's there all day …

The pages we have examined so closely would all have been written in the hour or so between the end of *The Archers* and repairing nightly to a local hostelry for a pint of beer. This was the pattern of Colin Dexter's writing for all thirteen of the Inspector Morse novels.

It is interesting to note, therefore, how many of the scenes of this first novel take place at about this time. It is largely a novel set at dusk.

The beginning of Chapter 5, for example, which was entitled originally *The First Witness*, demonstrates this same convergence of Art and Life as Mr. Bernard Crowther makes his way to the pub for his evening libation, as Colin Dexter would repair to the bar of The Friar Bacon, Cutteslowe, having finished work on the novel for the night.

[Banbury Road looking north toward Cuttleslowe and Dexter's house]

The parallels between Dexter's fiction and his own biography are evident still further in the manuscript of the novel where Crowther's house is described not as a detached but semi-detached (the qualification is scribbled through), like the house Dexter and his family moved to during the course of writing the novel, fronted by a small patchy strip (originally 'square') of lawn. Mrs. Crowther was 'disapproving' of her husband's nightly odyssey to the pub.

Crowther is an English don at an Oxford college which, initially, Dexter cites as Lincoln, appropriately enough since this is the county of his birth. Naming an actual college in a work of fiction is not, of course, tenable given the prominence one of its putative members of staff is to play in the story. Dexter therefore excises the name and makes several revisions. The manuscript shows 'Lon' first of all, an abortive attempt at the name he would eventually give to the college. Other contenders are 'Cowley' and 'St Edward's' before he settles on 'Lonsdale'.

Crowther's methodical – perhaps pathological – need for order and routine seems both touching and futile in the face of the tragedy which is about to unfold. Dexter's revision of the tense of the verbs, from perfect to conditional ('would turn' for 'turned right') also begins to cast an already retrospective shadow as though that period of his life is already over.

His destination in the published novel is the lounge bar of the Fletcher's Arms, though in the manuscript, the pub is named The Friar Tuck, a variation, of course, on the Friar Bacon, Dexter's own local.

Outside the garden gate, Crowther pauses for several (in the manuscript 'a few') seconds before turning left rather than right.

We can see that the gambit Morse plays in a previous chapter, relayed by the means of a television appeal for witnesses, has paid off, prompting Bernard Crowther's exodus. His resolution to come clean with what he knows is frustrated, however, by the fact that the call box is occupied by a 'portly' woman (she is described as 'middle-aged' initially in the manuscript). The woman, Dexter writes originally, appeared 'to be ill-equipped to face the triangular threat of the gadgets of the apparatus before her, an unco-operative operator and her own one-handed negotiations with the coins from her purse. But she was putting up a dogged fight'.

Generous momentarily in his impatience, Crowther wonders whether the woman is troubled for the well-being of one of her children, her husband unable to help because he is on the night shift. Significantly in the manuscript, Dexter adds the detail 'up at Cowley' but this is excised. Possibly the writer realised that this speculation on Crowther's part would mirror, then, exactly the situation of Sylvia's own parents. It remains an interesting parallel, however.
'But was her call really so important as the one he would make' Dexter originally wrote.

For it is in response to the item he had seen on the nine o' clock news (BBC is an addition in black ballpoint) that Crowther needs to avail himself of the closed confessional of the call box.

Colin Dexter almost overplays his hand at this point, however, in stating what it is that Crowther could tell 'the inspector'. He writes 'for he, Bernard Crowther had taken a hand'. This is amended to 'played his part' in the events 'that had led to Sylvi ...' To name the girl in this way and to use the verb 'taken' is to put Crowther in the driving seat, both literally and metaphorically. Dexter's alteration to his script wrings subtle changes and does not give too much away at this juncture.

35

'But what should he tell them?' Dexter originally wrote, summarizing Bernard's predicament very well. With the 'wretched' woman in the telephone box still not budging, Crowther decides to give her another minute, '60 seconds, no more' as the manuscript puts the ultimatum. This act of transference neatly projects any moral culpability onto an innocent party. The comment Dexter interpolates in the manuscript cuts through such casuistry: 'His fragile resolution began to crumble.' This is a theme to which the writer will return on the don's journey home.

Crowther's drinking partners at The Fletcher's Arms go unnamed in the published novel, but in the manuscript one, at least, is christened. Absent, too, is the conversational billiards, the words knocking together simultaneously like wooden balls as the men greet each other at the bar. 'The usual?' Colin Dexter writes initially, then 'What's it to be?'

 '"Oh, hello, Billy. Ready for another jar?"
 "What's it to be?"
 "Bitter, please," said Bernard.'

These exchanges are expunged in the published novel, the scene in the bar taking little more than half a page, its perfunctory nature perhaps reflecting Crowther's abstraction. By 10:25 pm he had, as the manuscript has it, 'polished off' three pints of bitter. The published novel offers the less colourful alternative 'He had drunk three pints of best bitter,' after which he makes his excuses and gets up to leave.

 '"You mean you're in the dog house again?" said Bill.
 "I'm always in the bloody dog house," laughed Joe.'

The sudden change of Crowther's Christian name from Bernard to Joe is interesting here. It may have been an alternative which the author at some point may have been giving serious consideration. It is expunged here, though, although with it, we also lose his laughter. Clearly, and despite imbibing three pints of beer, the contention is a sobering one. In what spirit does Crowther make this comment? Couched as it is in fairly bellicose language, it is nevertheless, perhaps, as near to a plea of mitigation as Crowther feels himself able to lodge.

The reader can perhaps conclude from all of this that it is not just his nightly sojourns down the boozer which leads his wife to find him 'errant'. They certainly do not comprise sufficient grounds to explain his tortuous progress home. Dexter delineates the topography of his craven indecision mercilessly, comparing his contortions to those of a small boy racing a car to the nearest ('next' in the manuscript) lamppost. Again, such childish superstition is merely an attempt to absolve himself of all responsibility. The pact he makes with himself – if Margaret is in bed, he will go in but if she is still up watching a television programme, he will ring the police – resolves itself to his immediate satisfaction and the reader's – hungry for more information – frustration. Dexter writes in the manuscript:

'He turned into the road and could see immediately that Margaret had gone to bed.'

The final words are excised and Dexter substitutes the phrase 'the bedroom light was on.' He will have to go in; the decision to contact the authorities is deferred and so, too, is the reader's gratification in discovering the English don's secret.

Dexter returns to the Crowthers' domestic situation in Chapter 8 which, prior to the writer's decision to simply entitle each chapter with the date was called *Mrs. Margaret Crowther & family.*

The chapter was prefaced originally in the manuscript with the Latin inscription *Non Sum Qualis Eram Bonae Sub Regno Cynarae,* (*I am not as I was ...*) appropriated by the minor Victorian poet Ernest Dowson and this contention lies behind much of Chapter 9.

In the opening sentence, the English don is named Joseph. Colin Dexter corrects himself, crossing out what was clearly his first choice and correcting it to Bernard.

The sentence as it originally appeared read:

'Joseph Crowther's wife Margaret disliked the weekends, and contrived matters in such a way to see that neither her husband nor her two daughters ...'

The phrase 'two daughters' is amended to '... twelve year old daughter nor her ten year old son liked them much either', the Crowthers' domestic situation, a son and a daughter mirroring, consequently, perhaps significantly, Colin Dexter's own. It is certain, however, that the state of Bernard's marriage, his day beginning as Dexter writes in the manuscript at one point with the don and his wife 'facing each other', in the original manuscript version, as though across a 'long-disputed frontier' does not reflect the Dexters' own marital union.

In a scene later in the novel, the children, James and Caroline (who was originally called Jennifer. The name is scored through since it had, of course, already been given to one of the novel's central protagonists) reflect on the state of their parents' marriage.

37

'The children were alone,' Dexter writes, adding this detail to the manuscript in green ink, perhaps to emphasize their isolation from their parents and the consequent uncivilized way they therefore treat each other.

'They hardly talk to each other,' the boy says of his parents.

His sister replies, in a phrase expunged from the published version:

"'Can't be lovey dovey all the time."
"Didn't used to be like this." (her brother says)
It was as long as most of their conversations ever lasted.' (Dexter writes)

Their conversation descends into squabbling and mutual recrimination, as conversations between children are wont to do. The reader can only speculate whether the scene was inspired by his own children's fractious arguments on that rainy day in Wales, which resulted in Colin locking himself away in the kitchen and beginning to work on what would become *Last Bus To Woodstock*.

Despite a part time job in the School of Oriental Studies (Dexter places her originally in a job in the 'University ...' but his ruling through the next word makes it illegible so her original occupation is difficult to determine), Margaret Crowther is, nevertheless, expected to wait upon her husband and their brood hand and foot. As Dexter describes the situation originally:

'The weekends, they all supposed were times of well-earned relaxations; but Margaret couldn't relax.
"Isn' there anything else?" had been the children's first response when she had 'given them poached eggs for tea' and while she is now all but chained to the kitchen sink. The children were glued to the television and wouldn't budge for the rest of the evening.'

Little wonder that Colin Dexter writes 'She thought sometimes that she was going mad.'

Watching her husband pruning the hedgerow, Dexter writes:

'She wondered what he was thinking about. It wouldn't be the hedge, she knew that but she also knew that she couldn't ask him.'

In trimming these lines, as Bernard is trimming the hedge, Dexter cuts the word 'also' and we lose the phrase 'It wouldn't be the hedge, she knew that' but here we have the crux of their marital difficulties:

'The truth was, and Margaret had escried (the word appears in the published novel as 'descried') it dimly for several years now that they were drifting apart. Was that her fault, too? Did Joe (sic) realise it?'

Leaving Bernard was one option but, Margaret concludes, she 'would have to stick it out longer yet.'

It is at this point the writer begins to reveal that there is more to Margaret's melancholy than mere domestic dissatisfaction. Dexter wrote originally:

'Unless something tragic happened – or was it <u>until</u> something tragic happened? And then she knew she would want to be with him – in spite of everything. Joe had been deeply upset, she could tell that, and with bitterness in her heart she was glad about that. What would he do?'

Much of this section is scored through and does not make the final version. Perhaps Colin Dexter felt there was too much enigmatic information for the reader; it was too long a pre-amble before he revealed the truth of the matter: that Margaret knew there was 'another woman.'

In place of this insight into her thoughts, Dexter cleverly patches in some lines of verse. Poetry is clearly very important in this highly literate household. Margaret has already made passing reference – appropriately enough since the novel is set in early October – to Keats's *Ode to Autumn* when she 'wondered, like the bees if these warm days would never cease.'

Now, 'after finishing the washing up', she goes through to the dining room and picks up the book Joe (sic) has been reading that afternoon: *The Collected Works of Ernest Dowson.*

Dexter writes:

'She remembered his name vaguely from her school-certificate days and she turned slowly through the poems until she found the lines they had all had to learn.'

The verse bears repeating here:

I cried for madder music and for stronger wine,
But when the feast is finish'd and the lamps expire,
Then falls thy shadow, Cynara! The night is thine;
And I am desolate and sick of an old passion,
Yea, hungry for the lips of my desire:
I have been faithful to thee, Cynara! In my fashion.

How apposite they are at this point in the novel, their inclusion a beautiful touch. For certain, the search for 'madder music and stronger wine' has been the undoing of many a man, Bernard Crowther, the first of them in the Morse novels. So, too, apart from providing Cole Porter with the title of one of his songs, is the last line a tantalising clue to the realisation at which Margaret has arrived. The sentence 'Of course Bernard could tell her all about it' is wonderfully ambiguous, referring not only to Crowther's literary ability to provide some sort of critical exegesis of the lines but also to explain the exact nature of this qualified fidelity he has kept after a fashion.

Perhaps the most touching and, in Margaret's case, the most flattering interpretation that can be put on the lines is that despite the temptations presented variously by wine, women or song, their pleasures have since turned to ashes in his mouth now Bernard has placed himself beyond his wife's grace.

Dexter writes, in the original version:

'She read them again and for the first time seemed to catch a glimpse of their magical meaning.'

All of which is only a prelude to the simple but quietly devastating sentence:

'It must have been an awful strain for Bernard meeting another woman once a week.'

It is what Colin Dexter first calls 'the horrible tension and agony', then 'the agonising tension and misery' and finally 'the tension and deceit' of the past four days (that is, since Sylvia was murdered on the 29th September) which has crystallised her suspicions, hardening them into certainty. In the process, she has traced the sourness from which her life seems to be suffering to its source. Suddenly, the bitter wife and cold, diffident mother becomes a much more sympathetic figure and the circumstances surrounding her husband's involvement with the dead girl a much more intriguing part of the mystery. How had his actions on that evening betrayed his secret to his wife?

It is clear from the desultory and trivial conversation which follows that neither partner is making any sort of explicit acknowledgement in front of the other about the truth of their situation. The conversation read, in the first instance:

'Joe came in. "God, my arms ache!"
"Have you finished the hedge?"
"I'll finish it off in the morning. It's those shears. I shouldn't think they've been sharpened for years."
"You could take them in."
"Yes, and get 'em back in about six months."
"You exaggerate."
"Never mind. ... Have you seen the lawn? It's like the Abyssinian desert."
"You've never been to Abyssinia."

The conversation dropped. Joe went to the bureau and took out the writing pad.'

Margaret's candour in confessing her indifference to her brood prompts some contrition from her husband but his promise of support only exacerbates her.

As she sobs in her room, Crowther realises 'He would have to do something and he would have to do it fast. He'd been a fool, a criminal fool! And now he was in real danger (now) of losing everything. He might even have lost it already ... But what could he do?'

Colin Dexter quotes further from Dowson, the lines illustrating the self-reproach which often heralds the morning after the night before ...

Surely the kisses of her bought red mouth were sweet;
But I was desolate and sick of an old passion,
When I awoke and found the dawn was grey:
I have been faithful to thee, Cynara, in my fashion.

Dexter wrestles with the expression of the thoughts these lines prompt in his protagonist. They are amplified more in his first attempt than in the version which appears in the published novel but this extended paragraph is scored through several times and the paragraph, as printed, is written out on a loose paper.

Dexter's first attempt at this interior monologue, however, reads:

'Yes, it had been sweet enough, it would be dishonest to pretend anything else but how sour it all tasted now. Should he go up to Margaret and tell her? No he couldn't. He realised that he would have been ... And what a relief it would have been to have finished with it all long ago with all the sordidness, above all with all the deceit. How fluent (a) liar he had become during this last year, but the tension and strain had sapped morale. He now knew that he was not a man who could ever again enter with any wholehearted vigour into the temp (tation) and yet how beguiling had been the prospect of extra-marital delights. But he had been long in learning/so slow in learning the simplest lesson but his conscience had been nurtured in a sensitive school. Fatal.'

Whilst the published version of this paragraph is much more polished – not to say florid in some of its metaphors ('... to have broken free from the web of lies and deceit he had spun about himself'), the rather more uncompromising vocabulary Dexter uses in this first draft – 'sordidness' – carries a more powerful charge. Such language takes no prisoners and the reader gets a much stronger sense of the character's self-reproach.

The lines 'How fluent (a) liar he had become during this last year, but the tension and strain had sapped morale' also demonstrate a keen understanding of the debilitating toll living a lie can exact.

A further casualty of Dexter's judicious self-censoring at this point is the sentence 'Should he go up to Margaret and tell her?' Despite reaching the conclusion that no, 'he couldn't', Dexter still excises the expression of Bernard's central dilemma.

Of course, on one level, this is a very necessary excision. Had Bernard confessed his transgression at this point, the novel may well have been considerably shorter and, in any case, this knowledge cannot be brought to light until certain other aspects of the solution to the mystery are in place.

Retention of these lines, however, would perhaps have rendered the relationship of the final four sentences to the rest of the paragraph a little clearer. 'Conscience. Damned conscience,' Crowther muses in the published novel. This seems to be something of a non sequitur with the thoughts that preceded it. On the face of it, Crowther seems to be bemoaning the fact that it is nurturing a moral sense of right and wrong which is the cause of his discomfort (an extremely egotistical position to take – none of his ruminations are on the effect his infidelity will have on his wife). The use of the word 'conscience' in this context is perhaps closer to that of Shakespeare in Hamlet's soliloquy in Act Three, Scene One. Here, Hamlet reflects, famously that '… conscience doth make cowards of us all'.

The word here means introspection rather than the moral sense of the difference between right and wrong. It is not that Hamlet thinks killing Claudius is wrong; it is simply that Hamlet thinks too much full stop. Possibly the Danish Prince is, therefore, articulating the very same indecision which afflicts Bernard Crowther here. It is, then, such a shame that we lose the line 'Should he go up to Margaret and tell her?' That is the question!

And just as, in the case of Hamlet, it is less doing the right thing than suffering the consequences, such considerations are exactly the reason Bernard procrastinates, too, at this point. What will happen to me if Margaret finds out? Dexter, therefore, shows the self-lacerating nature of Bernard's interior monologue and the extent to which he is the prisoner of his egotistical concerns for his own welfare. The published version is more polished but less powerful. In the manuscript, Dexter allows us a glimpse into the squirming vacillations of a tormented psyche.

As Bernard dwells on the 'Pauline assertion' that 'the wages of sin is death', we see that the academic is, in fact, not so much Hamlet as his father-uncle Claudius, desperate for redemption but unable to make the confession that will bring this desired state. As Claudius so epigrammatically concludes:

'My words fly up, my thoughts remain below:
Words without thoughts never to heaven go.'

Worse, the promise of salvation feels now only an empty one: a zealot in his
youth, Bernard finds his faith compromised by the doubt which manifests itself in
middle age. In the original manuscript, Colin Dexter writes:

'But he couldn't pray these days – all that was empty barren land.'

Instead, the cynical academic reaches not for the language of the hymnal – he
promise that his sins 'shall be whiter, yea whiter than snow' – but for a line from
Hollywood.

'Whiter than snow, indeed!' Dexter writes in the novel. 'More like the driven
slush.'

In the manuscript, Dexter acknowledges the source of this aphorism, however:

'Even now he recalled with a wry smile the words of Tallulah Bankhead.
'Pure as driven slush'.'

Dexter writes originally, 'He walked to the dining room window …' but
decided it was not necessary to remind the reader of Crowther's location and
excises the words 'dining room'.
What follows reads initially in the manuscript as:

'Lights were on in most of the windows now. A few people walked past;
a neighbour was putting his car away. An L-driver was struggling to turn a
car around a few doors away and was gradually succeeding, though the line
of symmetry through MAC's self drive Ford rarely progressed more than
seven or eight degrees at a time …'

Whilst the gender of the learner driver is not originally specified, for the
published version he makes the learner female.

In addition to this reference to learning to drive, Dexter adds a significant detail
in the published version about the activities of the neighbour who is now 'taking
his dog to foul some other pavement …' The reader could be forgiven for thinking
this is an oblique reference to Bernard's activities – 'not on your own doorstep'.

Certainly, the combination of images, a young woman struggling to negotiate
the public highway and a man seeking to discharge his dirty work farther afield
than his own neighbourhood, offers a symbolic microcosm of the novel as a
whole.

Another subtle theme of the novel is interwoven, too, at this point: how closely connected is the Chief Inspector to his chief suspect. For as Bernard looks out through his dining room window, he sees Morse.

The characters are connected closely, too, ultimately, in the manner of their deaths.

'Morse was used to death' Dexter tells us in the manuscript version of the novel but the assertion is ruled through. Omitted from the published novel also is the qualification that Morse had liked Crowther 'in an odd sort of way'.

Crowther's reflections on Morse are an after thought, an arrow drawn in blue biro from a balloon of text at the top of the foolscap page leads down to the end of the paragraph which concludes 'That last time ...'

The last sentences of this additional paragraph are not published in the novel and yet they are to prove, twenty-five years later and in the conclusion of the final Inspector Morse novel, strangely prophetic. The paragraph read originally:

'Morse must have had his wits about him, but he hadn't been quite clever enough to see the whole picture ... He couldn't have told Morse the whole truth, of course, but he hadn't deliberately meant to mislead him. A bit, certainly ... He'd like to see Morse, though. Nice chap. They seemed alike in some ways, he and Morse. Perhaps in other circumstances they could have got to know each other, become friends.'

The final three sentences of this paragraph are not in the published version of the novel. Crowther and Morse are more alike than anyone would have ever known at that point, however: for Inspector Morse is eventually to perish on a lonely hospital bed from a heart condition at the end of his own life, his dying wish to leave one last message ...

In the manuscript, the doctor tells him '"It's over now". It seemed an oddly prophetic remark,' although Dexter excises these lines.

Crowther's own feet are as cold as stone and Dexter's reference to the don 'babbling no more o' green fields' a Shakespearean allusion to the death of John Falstaff.

Part Five

Bras and Bars

$\mathbf{T}$he original title, written in the manuscript version for Chapter Three of the novel itself was *Bras and Bars*, recurring themes within the novel so far.

In the published version of the novel, the public house to which Lewis repairs at the end of the first full day of their investigation in search of his erstwhile boss is The Minster. In the manuscript, it was named for an actual public house in the city centre – which would be situated not too far from the Town and Gown Assurance Company of the novel on The High, The Mitre.

A listed building, The Mitre was established in 1261 and stands on the corner of The High and Turl Street.

Much to the sergeant's dismay, the Chief Inspector's efforts since they last met have revolved less around the murder investigation than around that morning's copy of *Sporting Life*, Morse weighing up the possibilities of backing a horse at 10 to 1 called The Black Prince. Is this really an appropriate use of police time?

[The Mitre, thinly disguised as the Minster in the novel]

Morse waives any consideration that what he is doing might be 'illegal' and encourages his sergeant to back the horse, too.

Morse says, in the manuscript version, 'Let's be bold, good sergeant. We going to (sic) back this horse to win, my friend.'

In the published version, Morse simply says to the sergeant 'You'll kick yourself if it wins' thus encouraging Lewis so to place his bet.

The pay off for this little exchange occurs in the following chapter when, the next morning, he duly tells Lewis that whilst the erstwhile sergeant has lost his money on The Black Prince, the Chief Inspector managed to save his own, and indeed even consolidate the investment a little, by doing precisely the opposite of what he had advised his sergeant to do: back the horse each way. The fact that Morse's finances are not at all compromised makes Lewis's conciliatory 'Better luck next time' of the manuscript even more touching. Dexter, however, wrings every drop of comedy he can out of the exchange. The offending nag is first referred to by Morse as the 'bloody thing.' This is scribbled through in the manuscript and the phrase 'miserable camel' is substituted before the writer finally settles on the much more pointed and comically satisfying alliteration of the 'constipated camel.'

The sergeant obviously finds Morse's conduct rather disconcerting and the extent to which he is perplexed by the Chief Inspector's behaviour is emphasized much more in the original manuscript. Despite the fact that he should be in a better position than anyone to understand his superior officer, it seems that everyone at the station seems to know more about that the enigmatic inspector than Lewis. When asked about Morse's apparent lack of punctuality, the desk sergeant replies 'Well, you know the Inspector'. Although not stated, Lewis's response to this in the manuscript is much more intemperate than it appears in the published version:

'"You obviously know more about him than I do," replied Lewis somewhat tetchily.'

Clearly in these early chapters of the novel, Colin Dexter is keen to portray Morse as, to quote Woodstock's most famous inhabitant, 'a riddle wrapped in a mystery inside an enigma'. With his apparently irrelevant preoccupations – betting, bras and bars – his stretches of indolence punctuated by sudden periods of frenetic activity, he is a completely unpredictable character whose words and actions manage to put Lewis on the back foot time and again.

Morse's occasionally querulous disposition and his cryptic sense of priority are evident in the four hours he and Lewis spend in Chapter Four sorting the reports.

'But I don't think I ...' Lewis is tempted to confess at one point in the manuscript, although the line is excised. He is puzzled, however, by Morse's apparently random preoccupations:

'"You seemed to find one or two of the reports very interesting, sir."
"Did I?" Morse sounded rather surprised.
"You spent about a quarter of an hour on that one from the secretarial college and it was its only half a page."
"You're very observant, sergeant Lewis, but I'm sorry to disappoint you. It was the most terribly badly ill-written report I've seen in years with twelve – no less – grammatical monstrosities in ten lines! What's the force coming to, Lewis?"'

Here is another illustration of Morse's apparently skewed priorities, the propriety of English syntax momentarily eclipsing the importance of finding the girl's killer. In an attempt to divert his superior officer's attention from his own grammatical inadequacies, Lewis re-iterates a question he seems forever to be asking the Chief Inspector:

"'Do you think we're getting anywhere, sir?'
"Doubt it'"

This is the same counter-productive retort with which the chapter closes and which may explain, in part, Morse's present sourness. It is also, perhaps, yet another mischievous attempt by Colin Dexter to subvert the form and expectation of the detective novel.

That same relationship between master and pupil, with Morse the pedant attempting to prompt the correct answer from his student, characterizes the rest of their subsequent conversation. Despite his reservations that the investigation is going nowhere, Morse's main concern is to establish the means by which Sylvia got somewhere on that fateful evening.

The fact that Sylvia had spaghetti Bolognese for her tea is a detail in the manuscript which does not make the final version of the novel nor does the reference to 'a white blouse' which is scored through in manuscript and the phrase 'the clothes in which she was found' substituted. That she left the house at roughly 6.30 and somehow got to Woodstock, seems, despite Morse's apparent pessimism, to be a 'decent' – amended to 'promising'– enough starting point for their inquiries – with the bus company, perhaps.

'It's clear … She didn't go by … I don't think she went by bus.'

To the proposition that a taxi might not be all that expensive, Morse simply repeats his blunt assertion that such an option is 'improbable.'

The exact terms of this improbability are expanded upon in greater detail in the manuscript in lines which are subsequently expunged. In response to Lewis' contention that 'It might not be all that expensive', Morse replies:

'We shall have a report this afternoon telling us exactly how expensive it is.'

Colin Dexter clearly decided that such circumstantial evidence was not necessary for the Chief Inspector to prove his point and the line was therefore cut, no such details ever being proffered in the case.

Asked how Lewis thinks the girl got to Woodstock, the sergeant initially replies 'Get a lift with a friend'.

Whilst the published novel tells us that Lewis 'wrote' the report, Dexter's first version says 'You've read the reports'. The revision only emphasizes the sergeant's obtuseness on this point.

Sylvia's apparent lack of girl friends precluding such a possibility, Lewis then says:

> '"What about a boyfriend?" Almost immediately Lewis could have kicked himself.'

This line is also deleted from the published novel. It is a little ambiguous: does Lewis wish to kick himself because the suggestion is ridiculous or because he wishes he had thought of it sooner? The possibility would certainly seem to contradict, or at the very least confuse, what we have already seen. If Sylvia was escorted to The Black Prince by a boyfriend, then this seems to ignore the presence of John Sanders in the pub who, it has been established, was clearly waiting for Sylvia to arrive. Little wonder that Morse demolishes the suggestion with his account of the interview he conducted with Mrs. Kaye (first 'yesterday evening', then 'early this morning' before Dexter finally fixes the time of the interview as 'last night') who saw her daughter walking away from the house unaccompanied and who, perhaps significantly, Morse believes found her daughter 'something of a trial'. Indeed, Colin Dexter puts this even more strongly in the manuscript when Morse says 'In fact I got the idea she wasn't over fond of her beautiful daughter'.

Lewis says simply 'Oh'.

Despite this, his superior officer seems rather favourably impressed by Mrs. Kaye who seems to bearing up well under the strain of events and who is in possession of a pair of 'broad shoulders'.

Possibly it is thoughts of Sylvia's mother which prompt the Chief Inspector to attend to his diminishing hair line, surveying himself in a mirror 'which hung over the/from his wall'.

He took out a comb and began 'to work on' his thinning hair in the manuscript which is amended to 'comb'. This makes a repetition of the word and, therefore, at some point Dexter – or his editor – amends the verb to 'groom'. The subsequent sentence originally read:

> 'He carefully drew a few straggling strands across a naked patch of hairlessness at the back of his skull.'

In the published version, we lose the rather effective adjective 'straggling', although this is re-inserted a couple of paragraphs later when Morse makes 'some

49

further passes at his straggling hair' and whilst 'broad' is a rather more effective substitute for 'naked', Dexter retains and even amplifies this word into 'nakedness'. The reader could be forgiven for thinking that the word 'bald' or 'baldness' would have been more apposite but this is not charged, perhaps, with the same meaning for our concupiscent Chief Inspector, reflecting perhaps still on the considerable assets of Mrs. Kaye.

Sergeant Lewis's reaction to Morse's 'grooming' goes unrecorded in the published version of the novel but in the manuscript, in response to Morse's unrecorded enquiry about his hairdressing, the sergeant replies:

'All right, I suppose.'

Morse's vanity continues to remain a theme until the end of the chapter. The contrast between his trivial preoccupation with matters tonsorial and the gravity of the dreadful circumstances of Sylvia's death, serves only to emphasize the bathos of the situation. When the cameras stop rolling, Morse's chief concern is 'that damned wind!' which has wreaked havoc on his pate. Such apparently unfeeling behaviour draws the reader's attention to the enigmatic nature of the Chief Inspector's skewed priorities and strengthens the conviction that the workings of Morse's mind are, ultimately, unfathomable.

In contrast, the workings of Lewis's mind are clearly audible. During this little tutorial on Sylvia's mode of transportation to the Black Prince two evenings earlier, one can almost hear the cogs revolving until, finally, a Damascene light dawns on the road to Woodstock:

'She must have hitched it, sir.'

Morse and Lewis have, therefore, arrived at the revelation with which the reader has been familiar since the Prelude. Such a public method of transportation must surely mean that somebody must have seen something. To go public with some sort of televised appeal is, then, the most obvious and logical course of action. The reader knows that such a public appeal may certainly reach Sylvia's anonymous friend at the bus stop and Mrs. Jarman, too. At least one more person would have some information: the driver of the vehicle in question, of course.

'"That is why"', Morse tells Lewis, in the manuscript, '"I would like to/must put in a little TV appearance tonight on the telly (tonight)." He picked up the phone and rang through to Scotland Yard put through a call to the Chief Superintendent (sic).'

It is fascinating to see that Colin Dexter originally intended to connect Morse to Scotland Yard. Despite the fact that the novel was published in 1975, one can almost see the trilby-hatted and mackintoshed officers, their black Marias, one steady bell ringing as a siren, drawing into Oxford at Morse's call. Dexter evidently thought better of it, however, deciding that the Chief Superintendent, and a man who was to feature with increasing prominence in the novels as the series developed, was a high enough authority to sanction such a broadcast, the time of its transmission fixed initially, in the manuscript, as Friday morning and then amended to Friday evening.

The word Colin Dexter uses originally to describe Morse's address to the nation is 'informed'. This is amended to 'appealed for help'.

There is information Morse clearly wants to communicate, however: the explicit circumstances of Sylvia's death. A very interesting point is raised here, however, between the version in the manuscript and that of the published novel.

There is a note in the margin of the manuscript on the previous page that says 'Med Report' which is then scribbled through – a reminder to himself from the author perhaps. As a result, Dexter originally included additional sentences which read:

'For the first time too Morse informed the nation of something he himself had known since the early hours of Thursday morning: the police/that a post mortem examination on the dead girl/that the murderer of Sylvia Kaye was a/… would face the further charge of sexual rape/assault and rape.'

This entire section is then expunged. We can see from this extract the writer's numerous attempts to fashion an official version of the circumstances surrounding Sylvia's death that he then abandons altogether. Also lost in this excision is the notion that the official post mortem only confirms what Morse had suspected from the outset.

In presenting the circumstances of Sylvia's death to the public, Morse is addressing the dark heart of this case. It is perfectly acceptable for the writer to mislead the reader, strewing the path with as many red herrings as he chooses and this is all part of the game. To cite any sort of official medical report as evidence would be outside the rules of the game, however. Such a report could not prove that Sylvia had been raped because, as the dénouement of the novel reveals, she suffered no such assault before her death. Morse leaps to the conclusion that she has been raped and then murdered with nothing but circumstantial evidence. Given the condition of Sylvia's body when the murdered girl is discovered, this is not an unreasonable conclusion to reach. To present to the nation such speculation as hard fact, however, is the sort of cavalier and disingenuous behaviour we have already seen Morse exhibiting in the placing of a bet on the Black Prince. The Chief Inspector is not above making something of a gamble and this certainly helps to drive the drama of the story, making Morse such a compelling and unpredictable character.

Morse is quite deliberately raising the stakes and this is evident in the revisions to this part of the chapter which do make the final novel. Colin Dexter writes:

'Morse informed the nation that the police were looking for a very dangerous man who might attack again at any time; for the killer of Sylvia Kaye, when brought to justice, would face not only the charge of wilful murder but also the charge of sexual assault and rape.'

The chapter may well have ended on this note, Morse's brio written in blue biro up to this point. The removal of all reference to a post mortem or a medical report, thus allows the Chief Inspector to postulate his hypothesis as fact. Morse may truly believe this is what has happened but Colin Dexter's revisions mean that his belief is never put to any sort of scientific test. It is not what happened at all: this is the whole point of the sleight-of-hand which lies at the heart of the 'whodunit' – things are never as they seem. There is a huge and necessary gulf, of course, between what an author knows and what his characters think they know. This is particularly important in this genre of novel. Morse may or may not be deliberately misleading his public but Colin Dexter certainly is.

And what Morse is up to consists of an attempt to flush the murderer out. This is made clear by an additional paragraph, written in the manuscript in black ink, and with which the chapter actually concludes.

The final words of the paragraph flatly contradict Morse's public assertion that the 'very dangerous man ... might attack again at any time.'

'Do you think he might really kill someone else, sir?' asks Lewis.

'Doubt it very much' says Morse.

This may seem a somewhat counter-productive assertion when there are over two hundred pages of the novel still to read. That there is a direct connection between the 'sex crime' and the death of the girl, to the extent that the same man perpetrated both, Morse seems to be in no doubt. His cavalier attitude towards such trivialities as forensic evidence is informed by his conviction in the leaps of his own intuitive imagination. It is the nature of that connection that Morse wants to test: why did the murderer behave in the way he did? By painting him as some sort of homicidal maniac, Morse is engaged in some game of brinkmanship. Not wishing to be tarred by such a brush, the murderer may well confess to what he has done, perhaps, as is often the case when criminals confess, hoping for a more lenient punishment. Like a teacher hoping an errant schoolboy might own up to a lesser crime if a greater is named Morse hopes that his television appeal might prompt such a confession from the murderer. The reader is prompted to keep turning the pages not by the promise of more grisly deaths but by wondering whether this compelling and enigmatic detective's gamble pays off.

Morse's egocentricity, to say nothing of the dispassion with which he seems to view the case, is apparent in the way he refers to his televised appeal for witnesses in a phrase struck from the manuscript. Asked by Sergeant Lewis the following evening if Morse would like to come with him to interview a witness who has come forward as a result of Morse's broadcast, Morse says:

'No ... I've done my party-piece for today. I don't want to come.'

Dexter qualified Morse's resolution in the original draft with 'But he went'.

The phrase would seem to indicate that the novelist originally intended to leave the scene there, perhaps deferring the revelation of a second girl who made that fateful journey towards Woodstock until the interview scene itself. However, this morsel is disclosed here in the scene, and the presence of 'this other girl' ('"What other girl?" snapped Morse') piques Morse's curiosity sufficiently for him to exchange his slippers for a pair of shoes.

When the two policemen arrive at Mrs. Jarman's, Morse's initial reluctance to be involved in the interview is reflected in his allowing Lewis to conduct the conversation. With uncharacteristic generosity in the manuscript, Morse acknowledges that, tedious though it is going over the events of the night in question, as far as the Chief Inspector was concerned, Lewis is 'his master here'. The version which appears in the published novel is the much less effusive phrase 'Lewis was doing it well'.

In any case, Morse proves himself still the master, extracting vital information even after Lewis believes the interview is at an end, the sergeant's 'self' satisfaction of the manuscript being moderated to 'mildly satisfied' for the published version.

In order to delay their leaving, Morse asks the woman for a cup of tea. Whilst she is in the kitchen, the policemen's exchange is a little more intemperate than in the published version of the novel, the late hour and incipient boredom perhaps taking their toll on Morse's capacity for patience:

'"Now listen. That bus. Get on to it."

"You mean tonight, sir?"

"I don't mean a week next bloody Tuesday, do I?"

Lewis got up.

"And," said Morse, "you've got that articulated lorry with the car bodies on it. We can trace that, with a bit of luck."

"Do you think we can?"

"I'm bloody sure I couldn't. But if you can't, God help you. You've got time – direction – what else do you want, man?"'

Much of Morse's unpleasantness here is excised from the final version, his admission that he would be incapable of tracing the lorry, similar to his lack of wherewithal to procure arc lights in Chapter Two, the Chief Inspector asserting clearly that such practicalities are beneath his attention and he has his mind on higher things.

Morse's sourness in the manuscript is returned in kind, however, by Lewis – in thought, if not in deed. Seeing his superior officer offered a drop of whisky from a bottle Mrs. Jarman has had – in the manuscript – 'for such a long time', Lewis is able to anticipate the likely outcome of his being proffered a drink – a re-run of the incident from Chapter Two. In the manuscript, Colin Dexter writes:

'Lewis smiled wanly. He knew exactly what was coming. He could almost mouth Morse's reaction.'

Being offered instead a cup of 'weak-looking' tea (it is described as 'wickedly dark brown' in the manuscript version), Lewis is equally as bitter and dismissive of Morse's attempts to be solicitous of Mrs. Jarman's health:

"'I hope you don't feel too tired?"
Smarminess itself, thought Lewis.'

Such mutual antagonism is toned down considerably in the published version. Indeed, in the case of the long-suffering sergeant, it evaporates almost completely in muttered, weary resignation.

As Mrs. Jarman looks for two whisky glasses, Colin Dexter writes:

'She fetched ... opened the ... a draw (sic) in the cupboard ...'

A hand, not Colin Dexter's own – perhaps his copy typist's – has written in black ink above the word 'draw' 'tut, tut!' Needless to say, the aberration is corrected in the published novel.

Back at headquarters, as is his wont, Morse conducts a little tutorial which originally opened with the following exchange:

"'Well, my friend?" Morse looked pleased with himself.
"You feel we're on the track, sir?"

"We are. Now tell me this. Let me test your powers of sifting evidence, sergeant.'"

Such a heavy-handed pedagogical approach is jettisoned in favour of the version which appears in the novel. So, too, is the qualification recorded a few lines later:

'Lewis tried to look intelligent but without much success.'

The contrast between Lewis's methodical and legitimate way of working and Morse's manipulative and cavalier ways is evident in their exchange over the niceties of obtaining a search warrant. Ignorance may be no defence but when that fails, Morse falls back on practicalities in order to get his own way:

'… perhaps you'll let me know where the hell I find anyone to sign a warrant at this time of the night – or morning, whatever it is.'

In lines subsequently expunged in the manuscript, Morse declines the offer of being accompanied by Lewis, moreover, ostensibly to protect his sergeant's sensibilities:

'In any case I couldn't let that lily-white mind of yours get besmirched with the depravities of our fellow human beings.'

Morse subsequently confesses: 'We're a despicable lot, us men aren't we?'

This rare lapse in the accuracy of the Chief Inspector's grammar is excised from the final version of the novel. The predatory nature of the male of the species, to which Morse alludes here, is often the defining characteristic of his investigations: the majority of suspects in the Inspector Morse novels are men and men, moreover, whose judgement is found wanting. Chief amongst them, as subsequent events in this first novel prove, is Inspector Morse himself. His assertion at this point, then and his professional desire to pursue and interrogate motive, are never more apposite.

The brief hiatus in the investigation at this point, however, both demonstrates the writer's sense of irony (and his complete control over his material, paying out the clues and playing with the constrictions of the genre) and, more importantly, allows the relationship between the Chief Inspector and his sergeant – such a large part of the Morse novels – to develop:

'"You could do with a pint of beer, sir".
Morse grinned in spite of himself.
"I suppose so."'

The dynamic of the relationship is slightly different at this point, however as an exchange which did not make the final version of the novel shows:

> "'Would you have picked them up?'
>
> "I don't usually, sir. Only if they're in uniform. I was glad of a few lifts myself when I was in the forces."
>
> Morse reflected carefully on this new evidence. It was certainly something.
>
> "What were you in, Lewis?"
>
> "I was a sergeant in the Signals, sir."
>
> "Oh, dear," said Morse "they didn't even promote me to Lance Corporal. It's a depressing morning.'"

Lewis's superior ranking to Morse in the armed forces puts the tin hat on it. Dexter clearly didn't want to put his chief creation down to that extent, maintaining instead the superior officer's superiority in all respects and this conversation was not included. It is no surprise, then, that Lewis's military rank was never revealed. Morse's response, nevertheless, is retained:

> 'What did you say about a pint?'

Whilst in the published novel, the name of the hostelry to which Morse and Lewis repair is given as the White Horse in Kidlington, in the manuscript it is referred to as the Black Horse. Perhaps, again, like the amendment from the Mitre to the Minster, this is to disguise the fact that such a public house exists.

In the manuscript, too, the phrase 'Morse assessed the beer was drinkable' is excised and replaced with the less pompous-sounding 'Morse decided that the beer was drinkable.'

Dexter writes:

> '... if alcohol was dulling the good sergeant's intellectual acumen, it had the opposite effect on Morse.'

Lewis is happy to be excused duties for the rest of the weekend, Colin Dexter supplying additionally that 'he had rested little and fitfully since the Wednesday evening of the murder, and was glad to have a brief respite from his duties. He left.' This information is excised from the final version.

Unrecorded too is the brand name of the packet of cigarettes Morse purchases. In the manuscript, Morse 'bought 20 Embassy'.

Alone – his characteristic and necessary condition - Morse is finally able to formulate the simple conundrum which lies at the heart of everything:

> 'What the hell had really happened last Wednesday evening?'

Rather then embark upon some beer-fuelled flight of fancy, making startling leaps of inspired intuition, the Chief Inspector seeks simply an 'ordinary' (amended to 'logical') progression: he is convinced that 'if only his mind could project itself into perfectly causal relationships, from A to B to C to D and to wherever' he would have the mystery solved. But each of the lines of thought he follows lead 'to a blank wall', then 'to nowhere' until Dexter completes his analogy to a puzzle in a child's annual by writing 'to the edge of the page'.

For Morse, this lack of a clear and logical crossword-like solution to the question is 'torment'.

The landlord's injunction, 'I'm afraid I shall have to ask you to drink up' only exacerbates the aridity of Morse's mind at this point and the Larkinesque sterility ('Nothing, like something, happens anywhere') that has characterized Morse's endeavours at this point in the unfolding plot.

Part Six

Education, Education, Education

When asked how he would like to be remembered, Colin Dexter replied:

'As a good teacher. I got more pleasure from teaching than any other job in my life.'[1]

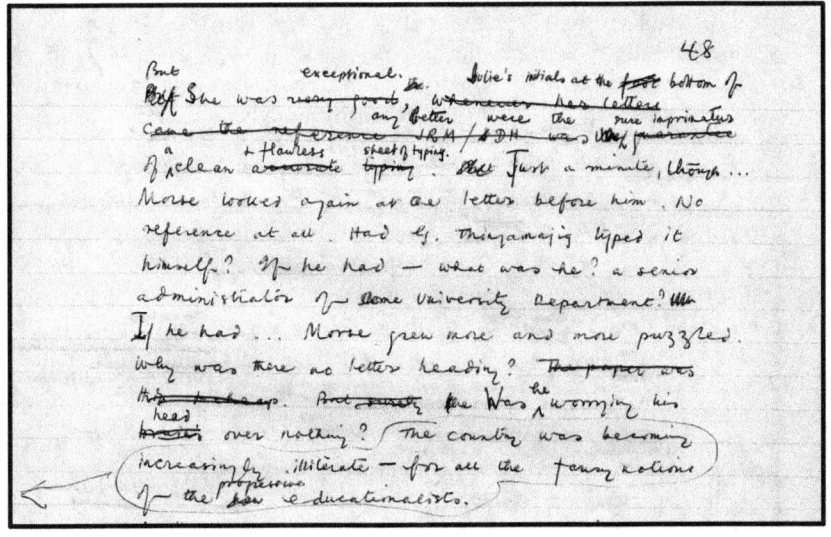

Dexter was a teacher of classics and considered himself always more a teacher than a writer. While head of classics at a school in Corby, Northamptonshire, he learned that his hearing had deteriorated to such a point that while teaching Book II of *The Aeneid*, he had not realised the fifth form were loudly playing pop

---

[1] *Author Colin Dexter: The Definite Article – Writer's Cut* by Rob McGibbon, 2014.

music in his lessons. He decided therefore to leave teaching and became an examiner for the Oxford University Board.

In Colin Dexter's obituary which appeared in *The Guardian*, Dennis Barker wrote:

'Dexter was often asked whether he wrote for a readership or for himself. His answer was that he wrote for his old English teacher Mr. Sharp. He would write a page and then ask himself, 'Would Mr. Sharp like that?' His aim was to feel that Mr. Sharp would give it at least eight out of 10.'[2]

Colin Dexter himself elaborated upon this theme in an interview with *The Guardian* in 2008, from which, in part, his obituary was possibly drawn. Dexter said:

'During the war years I was at school at Stamford in Lincolnshire. It was a boarding school but I was a scholarship boy from the town. Mr. H. B. Sharp was a senior English master who ran the school magazine and I caught his eye when I wrote an article about poetry for the magazine. Ever since I'd 'wandered lonely as a cloud' a few years earlier I had a more-developed sensitivity to poetry than my peers and so it was when I was 15, Mr. Sharp took me to one side and told me that he was going to write to my mother and father and ask them to cancel my weekly subscription to the *Dandy* comic. And that once a fortnight I was to come to his library at his home and choose a book.

… When I left school we kept in touch and it was then that I learned that his Christian name was Hugh, but quite rightly, I always addressed him as Mr. Sharp, while he called me Colin. He moved to the south of France when he retired and we always exchanged Christmas cards and he let me know that he'd read about Old Morse. I think in his own way he was proud of me although he never said that. I had to move house in 1973 and I found one of his books, *The Collected Poems of Yeats*, and I packed it up and sent it to him, 25 years after I'd borrowed it. Later I got a parcel back where he'd crossed out his name and put mine instead with a note underneath which read, 'Life is full of great surprises and I didn't think there were many left, but it's been a great surprise to learn late in life that you're such a slow reader'.[3]

On another occasion, Dexter recalled:

'(Sharp) used to read an essay of mine and say, 'Really not very good, is it? Could be better, couldn't it,' and I knew he was right. I think of him

---

[2] Colin Dexter obituary by Dennis Barker, *The Guardian*, 21st March, 2017.
[3] *My Mentor* by Deany Judd, *The Guardian*, 26th July, 2008.

when I write and when I finish a page I pray it is as good as it can be, so that Mr. Sharp would see it and he would say, "Well done, boy."[4]

The detective novelist's reticence over the use of the Christian name with his former teacher may well have played a part in Dexter's decision to keep Chief Inspector Morse's a mystery. It was clearly a policy from the outset. At the end of *Last Bus to Woodstock*, Sue Widdowson, suspect and sometime sweetheart of the detective says:

'Inspector, you never did tell me your Christian name.'

The analogy to teaching is made explicit in the novel also. The reader can only speculate on the number of occasions Colin Dexter met a former pupil. Was it these awkward social occasions that prompted Morse's thoughts on his first date with the young woman:

'He didn't know what to do about this name trouble. He felt like an ageing schoolmaster greeting/meeting one of his old pupils and being rather embarrassed by the 'Sirs' in every other sentence and yet feeling it phoney to have it otherwise.'

The most frequent use of the epithet 'sir' is of course made by Sergeant Lewis. Their relationship could indeed be characterized as that between master and pupil. The parallel is drawn quite specifically when Morse's case against his chief suspect seems on the point of collapse. It is a rare instance in their teacher and student relationship when Lewis has the advantage. 'When Lewis had turned on the car engine and sat with the window down, behind the steering wheel' Dexter writes, although he thinks better of it and rules through this sentence, Lewis feels like a pupil who has caught out his teacher first with what Dexter calls a 'tricky' spelling before amending this to the even more damning 'simple' word. Originally Lewis asks the Chief Inspector:

'Did you ever test it (the letter) for finger ... find any finger prints on it, sir?'

The way the question is asked could only compound Morse's misery still further. It is just as well that it is phrased a little more kindly in the subjunctive in the published version: 'Could there have been some fingerprints ...?' Little wonder, in response to the original phrasing, that Morse 'seemed to be staring' blankly. Dexter writes:

'He thought seriously that he should take up school teaching – primary school would be about his level; spelling, he thought, the safest bet.'

---

[4] George Raine, *The Examiner*, 1ˢᵗ June, 1995.

The influence of HB Sharp, however, is felt throughout the novel, Morse's approach to the case ever that of the pedantic schoolmaster.

Fiction and autobiography are confused quite happily across the end of Chapter 6 and the beginning of Chapter 7; Morse's own grey matter being inspired by alcohol in much the same way as the writer's in creating his fiction. It is undoubtedly Colin Dexter's experience as a teacher which fuels Morse's thoughts on bad grammar and spelling mistakes in the next few lines.

'... just look at those wretched misprints' Dexter wrote in the original version. 'No one in the schools cared much these days about the bread-and-butter mechanisms of English usage.'

'The schools' is a phrase which conjures Dexter's then present circumstances as an examiner in Oxford. Morse's memories that '... he'd been brought up in the hard school: errors of spelling, punctuation and construction of sentences had been savagely penalised by pedantic/by his outraged teachers/schoolmasters pedagogues(.) It and this had made its mark on him...' are clearly, also, Dexter's own.

The reader wonders, too, whether the exceptional secretary, Julie, of whom Morse thinks so highly when he reflects upon the ill-written report he had received 'the previous Thursday', is Dexter's own, too:
'She was very good/exceptional, whenever her letters came the reference JRM/DH was the guarantee of clean accurate typing.'

There is no actual example of an initialled reference in the final novel, but it is the lack of one on this letter which makes Morse begin to wonder about its veracity. Neither is there any sort of letter heading and, in the original manuscript, Dexter writes, 'The paper was thin and cheap. But surely he was worrying his head over nothing? The country was becoming increasingly illiterate – for all the fancy notions of the progressive educationalists.'

This final comment is ringed, an arrow drawn, indicating it is to be 'cut and pasted' at a more appropriate point in the paragraph.

Morse's frustration with 'progressive educationalists' is compounded by comments the author makes on the iniquities of contemporary student politics at university level. These were expunged from the final version of the text, however, not making the published novel.

They appeared originally at the end of a description of first year undergraduates exploring the bookshops of the Broad. This section was transposed from the beginning of Chapter Eighteen as a preface to Morse's shopping expedition to Marks and Spencer in the previous chapter. Dexter copies part only from the top of page 152 of the manuscript. The original paragraph is then crossed through and a green arrow drawn, indicating that the section has been moved. The entire description reads originally:

'Wednesday the 13ᵗʰ Oct was the third full day of the Autumn Term. First year undergraduates, spankingly new college scarves tossed over their shoulders, explored the book shops along the Broad and a trifle self-consciously strode down the High into the crowded Cornmarket with its ... into Woolworths and Marks and Spencer & thence according to tastes, into the pubs or the coffee shops. Sits in at the schools would not occur for several weeks yet, for the Summer smiled on with fresh open sunny days and the young men had not yet had their attention drawn to the wickedness of the university in having authorities in denying greater powers to the National Union of Students. Examinations seemed aeons ahead. Gather ye rosebuds while ye may.'

In his politics, Colin Dexter was progressive. He described himself as a 'lukewarm socialist'. As the election of a New Labour government approached in 1997, and some of the most wealthy threatened to leave the country over a potential rise in taxation, Colin Dexter's response was 'Let them! Let them!'

In terms of education, he was much more of a traditionalist. At the height of his fame, his photograph appeared prominently on the front page of *The Times Educational Supplement* in October 1992. He stood in quarter profile, his shadow in the autumnal sun cast against the cinnamon-coloured Cotswold stone of an Oxford college, looking pensively through the black iron railings of the college gates.

'I don't know how people can teach these days,' he is quoted as saying. 'They're just filling in forms all the time. These days everybody worries about the motivation of children to learn. When I taught they all wanted to learn. It was a lovely job which I enjoyed very much.' His romantic view of the profession and his vocation is emphasised even more in his belief, 'I think a good teacher can make the dead live. They talk a lot about the value of homes, and of course that is important, but if you had the choice I'd say a decent teacher is better for a child.'[5]

His perceived inadequacies of the English system of education continued to exercise him. 'Children don't know what a full stop is ... It's a public confidence trick to be told that standards at 16 or 18 are going up. The vast majority know

[5] Susan Young, *The Times Educational Supplement*, 16ᵗʰ October, 1993.

perfectly well that that is not true. When people say the evidence is only anecdotal, I often wonder what is wrong with anecdotal evidence.'[6]

Did Colin's former career as a pedagogue comprise the model for Morse's forensic deconstruction of a suspect's testimony? In this, the Chief Inspector's great literary forebear could as well be the pedantic and disbelieving Housemaster Le Bas in Anthony Powell's novel sequence *A Dance to the Music of Time* as Sherlock Holmes or Philip Marlowe. Certainly, the first interview with a suspect Morse conducts in *Last Bus to Woodstock* has all the hallmarks of an interrogation by an incredulous schoolmaster.

As a former classics master, versed in Socratic dialogue, this kind of dialectic would come easily to Dexter. There must have been many occasions when he had cause to cross-examine the veracity of a pupil's account of things and this – rather than any established police procedure – is surely Colin Dexter's model for tackling the interviewing of a witness. The first interview the reader sees Inspector Morse conduct is with the young man who had an assignation with Sylvia Kaye at The Black Prince.

When first asked his name, the witness replies: 'Sanders; George Sanders.'

Perhaps to avoid confusion with the late actor of the same name, Colin Dexter amends his first name to John.

And like a naughty schoolboy, John Sanders's economy with the truth in this scene is brought very sharply to book.

Evidently, in the first of those startling leaps of faith Morse makes throughout the novels, the detective assumes that the blonde girl Sanders was seen with in the pub the previous week is the dead girl and that Sanders was expecting to meet her there again that evening. It is an admission on the part of Sanders that these assertions are so that drives the interrogation.

Sanders initial claim that 'There's not much to tell, really' is greeted with knowing scepticism by the Chief Inspector, his rejoinder 'Then we needn't keep you long, need we, Mr. Sanders?' has the effect that 'The young man felt a little puzzled, fidgeted, ill at ease. Morse sat opposite him and looked him in the eye and said nothing, waited.'

There is a telling phrase and a very clever attitude struck by the young man at the end of his testimony in the original manuscript which, nevertheless, had it

---

[6] Dalya Alberge, *The London Times*, 19th April, 1997.

been retained in the final published version would still not have cut any ice with Morse:

'Well, sir, I just walked into the courtyard and there she was. I didn't touch her, but I thought she was dead. I went straight back in to see the manager and you know the rest.'

Dexter makes tiny amendments to this first attempt, the most significant and effective of which is to change 'I thought she was dead' to 'I knew she was dead', the word 'knew' super scribed in black ink. The phrase 'and you know the rest' is struck through entirely. The young man should be so lucky to get away with such an evasive utterance.

Until Morse questions him explicitly on the point, Sanders neglects to tell Morse that he had gone into the car park to be sick although how Morse knows he was, the reader is not told.

Sanders seems concerned to assert that he was sick after he had found the girl – 'sort of shock, I suppose' – but Morse insists on 'the truth':

'"You haven't got your car here have you?"
"I haven't got a car"' – the optimistic 'yet' is expunged in the manuscript, as is Morse's initial response to this: 'I saw I think …'

What Morse is driving at is that since Sanders does not have a car, he has no possible motive for being in the courtyard, unless it is to vomit but it is not easy to get Sanders to admit as much.

Morse has to struggle to get the simple admission from the young man that he had been drinking to excess, threatening to find out the truth from 'other witnesses' in the first version, then 'someone else', presumably Gaye McFee who did not, earlier, have the opportunity to tell the detective the extent of the young man's drinking.

This paragraph reads, originally:

'"Mr Sanders. Do you want me to find out from other witnesses how long you'd been drinking in the cocktail lounge?"
Clearly Sanders did not welcome any such enquiry.
"I came in at seven but I wasn't drinking all the time." The young man grew more ill at ease than ever. Sanders was still uncertain what to say.
"What time did you come in?" continued Morse.
"Seven – about seven."
"And you got drunk and you went out to be sick."
"Yes."'

In contrast to the final published version, 'Reluctantly Sanders agreed', the young man's simple affirmative is understated but quietly devastating and there are revelations of even greater import to come:

"'Do you often drink on your own like that?'"
"No."
"You were waiting for someone."
"Yes."
"She didn't show up?"
"No," said Sanders flatly.
"But she did come, didn't she?" said Morse gently.
"No, I told you, I was on my own all the time."
"But she did come, didn't she?" persisted Morse, coaxing and gentle.
Sanders said nothing. He looked tired and beaten.
"She came," continued Morse in the same quiet voice.
"She came and you saw her. You saw her in the courtyard, and she was dead."
"Yes.'"

Prior to Colin Dexter's revisions, the original version of the interview, even as it is set out on the page, is much more stark. There are neither obfuscations nor embellishments behind which Sanders can hide. He maintains the air of a generally sullen schoolboy, Morse's cross-questioning chipping away at the young man's carefully constructed defences until they finally capitulate in what amounts to an admission that Sanders knew the identity of the dead girl. Morse only has to push his advantage home.

It is for this confession that Morse has undermined the young man's various evasions: that his being sick was brought about by strong drink rather than strong feelings; that for whatever reasons of his own, when he returned to the bar and in his subsequent conversations with the police, he attempted to marginalise his knowledge of and involvement with the dead girl. This is the very stuff of a good detective novel, however. Dexter had already said: 'It was clear from Sanders' manner that he hardly welcomed an inquiry along such lines.' The reader can only wonder whether Sanders has proved so evasive simply to protect the sensibilities of his mother who 'though she knew he would expecting him to be late, would be (getting) worried' or whether there is something altogether darker about his motives.

In the original manuscript, a line of thought by Morse is left unfinished. Colin Dexter writes:

'Morse called Lewis. "Sergeant. Ge ..."'

The writer may have felt that a diversion at this point would simply draw the reader's attention away from what is the most significant development of the case so far: Morse is now in a position to discover the identity of the victim. The last line of the chapter first read:

'"Who is she?" asked Morse.'

This is excised and Dexter then writes:

'"You'd better tell me who the hell she is," said Morse.'

The final lines which appear in the published version of the novel, '"We'd better have a little chat, you and me," said Morse ungrammatically', are much more effective, however. In these lines, a great deal is implied: the young man's certain knowledge of the girl's identity and the tacit promise to the reader that there is much more to Sanders's story than he has so far confessed.

These final lines appear in the published version of the novel only, however. There is no version of them in the manuscript. At what point the lines were altered, therefore, can remain only a matter of conjecture; the whereabouts, and indeed the existence, of any amendment to this effect in Colin Dexter's own hand remain only a mystery.

Part Seven

Never a Crossword

It is not clear from which stage of the creative process the manuscript of the novel survives. All the revisions, corrections, addenda and errata demonstrate, however, that what survives in Colin Dexter's own hand is much more than a fair copy from which the typist could work. The revision and fine-tuning is exhaustive and extensive enough to be able to argue that what we see in the manuscript is a genuine work in progress.

It is all the more remarkable then that the iconic portrait of the Chief Inspector drawn in the first two or three pages of Chapter 9 shows little revision, apart from Morse's mind originally being described as 'wearied' rather than 'harassed'.

There is one major revision, however, which had it stood, would have changed our perception of Morse's tastes quite radically.

As Morse attempts to complete the crossword puzzle in that week's copy of *The Listener*, he listens simultaneously to a recording of Wagner's *Das Rheingold*. Morse is forever associated with the music of Richard Wagner and yet this was not Dexter's first choice of music. In the manuscript, he writes:

'... he delighted in the Schubert Lieder and had the complete set of the song cycles *Winter Reise*. He decided to do both, and with Fischer Dieskau ... pouring out his soul to si(ng)'

Ultimately, however, Schubert's Lieder is super scribed with 'Wagnerian opera' and *Winter Reise* with *The Ring*.

The substitution therefore completes what was to become the iconic image of Chief Inspector Morse, in repose, solving crosswords to the sound of his beloved Wagner. The picture seems to symbolize the character's essential isolation. Morse is a figure who is romantic in the widest sense of the word. Romance, in its more conventional guise, however, is offered as the solution to his solitude and solutions connected to a girl seem to offer themselves in this opening scene, too: any plans Morse might have had for a leisurely Sunday morning are hastily set aside as he realizes the acrostic pattern of the crossword is of direct relevance to the case.

'SAY NOTHING' is the result of this acrostic deception and, in the original manuscript although this fails to make the published version of the novel, Dexter appends this emphatic gloss on, Jennifer Coleby's response: 'She hadn't'.

'It was fortunate for Morse' Dexter wrote originally that Jennifer Coleby had been out the night before when he called because she could easily have claimed she was mistaken about her alibi. Now, with the acrostic clue, Morse has cast iron evidence of her involvement as a possible accessory. And yet, Dexter writes in a passage he subsequently excised, Morse 'had to admire her fiercely maintained loyalty even more.'

Nevertheless, at this stage in the novel, Morse is convinced that Jennifer Coleby, who worked in the novel with Sylvia Kaye at the Town and Gown Assurance Company, was the second girl at the bus stop. Certainly, Jennifer

Coleby was the name Colin Dexter started to inscribe in the original version of the Prelude before striking it through. A different character altogether, then and one for whom, we must assume Dexter had an entirely different name in mind already, was intended to be standing at the bus stop with Sylvia, a character whose significance to the mystery – and to Morse – would be far greater than Jennifer Coleby's.

Had the second girl been Jennifer Coleby, it would have been here, as Dexter put it originally, 'she had witnessed at least something which it was vital to keep to herself.'

Convinced that she knows the identity of Sylvia's murderer and therefore possibly in danger herself, Morse decides she must be 'arrested' in the original manuscript before this is changed to 'held on suspicion of being an accessory'.

The ensuing interview with Jennifer Coleby, who sits, in the manuscript version 'demurely', is written with little revision. A couple of lines only are excised: 'For the first time there was a hint of uneasiness in the tone of Jennifer's voice' and the assertion that 'He (Lewis) was doing well' perhaps because they give the impression that the Detective Sergeant is making rather more headway than he does and that Jennifer is discomfited ever before Morse makes his entrance. The effect of these excisions is to remove this impression. The original entrance of Morse on the scene was much more ominously expressed too:

'For rather more than ten minutes, Jennifer sat alone, watched over by a policewoman who appeared singularly uncommunicative. Then the door opened at last and a ... but the man entered with holding a neatly typed sheet of foolscap. It was not Sergeant Lewis', before it is ruled through with a single, wavy line in red ballpoint. Beneath this excision is written in red ink also, the passage as it appears in the published novel, the only amendment being the phrase 'When the door finally opened, it was not to admit Lewis.'

Morse's entrance ensures 'the tide of relaxation' ebbs and exposes – originally – the 'rasping' shingle of her nerves.

As the atmosphere between the Chief Inspector and his chief witness grows more tense, Colin Dexter writes that Morse raised his voice 'from p. to mf,' thereby grading finely the modulations in his vocal power from 'moderately soft' to 'moderately loud'.

Whilst the musical analogy here is abandoned, Dexter does return to it at the end of Morse's case for the prosecution when Dexter writes the Chief Inspector's voice 'had risen further throughout the speech', amending this to the phrase which appears in the published version, 'in crescendo'.

The logical conclusion to such a musical analogy – 'he ended on a shrieked falsetto' – is, however, struck, perhaps for hitting a note which is a little operatic, even for Morse.

In the original manuscript, Morse 'hoped' Jennifer would look abashed although this is amended to 'expected' in the published version. The disappointment of Morse's expectations is all the more pronounced when Dexter, further, excises any trace of misgivings or surrender on Miss Coleby's part:

> 'But although visibly shaken by his outburst, she was not giving in quite so easily as that.'

Far from being caught on the back foot, Jennifer wrests control of the conversation entirely from Morse in a comical reversal of roles.

Telling 'of his discovery' that her flawed alibi can be thrown out 'without any shadow of a doubt', Morse is, in the original manuscript, 'staggered' by her response as the young woman proceeds to ascertain the exact whereabouts of Morse himself on the evening in question.

Who was conducting this interview anyway? is a question Morse might well have asked himself at this point, except he had already asked it on their first encounter.

Of their first encounter, Dexter wrote originally:

> 'Jennifer spoke with an easy, clear diction. She'd had a good education, he'd bet. But there was more coolness than that.'

The cool Miss Coleby expresses surprise that the Chief Inspector hasn't interviewed those who worked with Sylvia much sooner, comments on the casual attitude he seems to display towards choosing his reading matter and even offers suggestions of works of literature he really ought to read.

Morse is suitably abashed, comments Dexter included in the manuscript but subsequently deleted indicating, perhaps, how much the Chief Inspector is taken with the girl's collected demeanour:

> 'She laid a delicately manicured hand lightly upon *Villette*.
> "Yes. Have you read it?"
> "'Fraid not" confessed Morse. Damn it, he ought to have done, but he felt he oughtn't to tell too many white lies to Miss Jennifer …

"You should do."

"I'll try to remember" muttered Morse. Who was conducting this interview anyway?'

Little wonder the Chief Inspector feels he is 'losing his way'.

Morse's original response to her account of her journey home on the evening of the 29th September is a little over-written and it is little wonder that Dexter excised it from the manuscript:

"'I got home about six, I should think. You know what the traffic's like in the rush hour."

"Alas, I do.'"

Over elaborate language is perhaps the last refuge of the diffident, however, Morse seeking to retreat into verbosity to defend himself from Miss Coleby's level gaze. Morse's conclusion originally that Jennifer 'was' very nice indeed is amended to the strictly conditional tense of 'could be'.

'What was he doing?' Dexter writes in the manuscript. 'He didn't know but such an admission would hardly befit the present interview.'

Of the bizarre turn the interview has taken, Dexter states originally much more baldly:

'He could not help himself, he admired the girl.'

She certainly wrong foots Morse. The conversation at this point originally ran:

"'You're a clever woman, Miss Coleby, and I hope you will allow a modicum of intelligence to the police."

"Shouldn't you be more worried about the man who murdered Sylvia?"

"Believe me, we are, but I've got to discover what happened ..."

Morse took the statement Jennifer had made and tore it into pieces which fluttered like ash-pods into the waste-paper basket.'

This action is not described so floridly in the published version of the manuscript, nor is Jennifer's reaction to the interrogative:

"'Well?"

The monosyllable appeared to jerk her back into the reality present.'

"You are right, inspector," Jennifer replies in the manuscript (rather than the apology – 'I'm sorry, Inspector' of the published version) and, again excised from the published novel she prefaces her new story with 'I remember it all now'.

Morse is no more impressed with Jennifer's revision of her alibi than he was with the original version to the extent that in the manuscript he asks her:

> "'Do you want me to arrest you as an accessory to murder?'
> His voice was exasperated and he furious.'

Dexter writes originally but …

> 'Jennifer appeared perfectly calm and Morse's anger had slowly subsided when Lewis appeared.
> "Take a seat, sergeant. Miss Coleby got things a bit muddled in her statement. We're going to start again."'

[The refurbished Kidlington HQ]

In fact, over the next two pages of the novel, Dexter mischievously sets up the punch line to the whole interview. Morse's new-found attraction to his chief suspect, Dexter originally writing 'Morse seemed to be looking at her for the first time' combined with the bathetic pay-off pre-figures the novel's larger conceit: that Morse falls for the charms of a young woman and is bested by his infatuation.

'I'm sorry to be so maudlin' is how Jennifer describes her confusion in the manuscript version of the later interview at Kidlington HQ.

Lewis is equally bewildered 'at the brevity of his notes – seven whole lines!' something of a clue that the Inspector was far more interested in the witness herself than in completing the administrative aspects of the task at hand.

The entire premise upon which Morse is building his case against Jennifer Coleby collapses however in the ensuing exchange. Attempting finally to ascertain the identity of the man who gave her a lift to Woodstock on the fateful night, Morse discovers that far from being the original second girl at the bus stop, Miss Coleby had no business being at a bus stop in the first place: *she has a car.*

Dexter places a much greater emphasis on Morse's equanimity in the face of his investigation stalling in the manuscript than appears in the published version; and this, despite the consequences of his failure being drawn even more starkly. Dexter writes originally:

'For some reason he felt far from depressed, although he fully realized that if he didn't come up with something fairly quickly then his immediate superior would want to know why/have little option but to call in the/ Scotland Yard.'

The fact that he had 'not taken up' the offer of auxiliary personnel, amounts, in the original manuscript, to 'an almost unforgivable negligence'. Indeed, the word unforgivable is scored through and the adjective 'criminal' applied, in its stead, in red ink.

Despite this, Dexter writes, 'that although his latest shot at goal had been kicked off the line, he still would score sooner or later, though perhaps not from the other wing.' The metaphor is re-worked considerably in the published version.

The officers exchange notes on the interrogation, Morse originally 'insisting on probing the minutest reactions, evasions, glances, words and gestures of Jennifer Coleby and then recounted to Lewis his own interpretation ...

'Let me tell you something then. When you're as old as I am you'll recognize a liar a mile off!'

Initially, Dexter simply writes at this point 'Lewis remained doubtful'.

Morse says originally 'Well half a mile' although this qualification is excised from the text.

In the novel, Dexter writes of Lewis:

'He was a few years his inspector's senior in age.'

Nevertheless, Morse casts himself as the paternal figure when he says:

'A wise man hears his father's instruction, Lewis. Book of Proverbs – somewhere.'

In the original manuscript, Lewis's verdict on the state of their investigation so far and, signally, in taking the word at face value of the landlady who recognized Jennifer Coleby is:

'It wouldn't stand up in court, would it?'

The redoubtable Sergeant Lewis then exits. Dexter writes 'End of Part One' but changes his mind, scribbling through the legend and continuing with further speculation on Morse's part about Jennifer's motives, Dexter writing originally:

'Perhaps, after all, everything she had told him was absolutely true. But what happened after that her story ended? Morse did not yet know or, rather, he knew/did know one fact. Sylvia Kane had been murdered.'

Part Eight

Not a line of her writing have I …

Colin Dexter writes originally that Jennifer Coleby rented with three other 'working girls' (a quaint phrase which rather dates the prose) before amending this to two. The address at 36 Temple (Temple Road is in Cowley, some 15 minutes' drive away from the Banbury Road) 44 'which hung over the/from his wall'.

'The landlord had 'forbidden' men friends in the bedroom', although the quotation marks which appear in the manuscript around the injunction are absent in the published text.

Dexter continues with a phrase which is also excised from the final version:

'... and oddly enough the girls ... considered this a fair request.'

In the published novel, this whole phrase is re-written as:

'... the girls had accepted his Diktat without contention.'

It is a shame to lose the phrase 'oddly enough'. Given the behaviour of two of the three housemates, such abstinence from the company of men is indeed odd, although their exclusion from the premises may help to explain why the girls had to seek their society where they could find it.

Dexter records the fact that there had been a few 'infractions' of the ban but the girls' home had never degenerated into 'a haven for promiscuous young men' (or into 'overt promiscuity' as the final version reads, an alternative which, on balance, seems rather more fair to young men. It does, after all, and as the novel proves, take two to tango).

The girls' only self-imposed stricture is 'no gramaphone (sic)', which is amended in the published text to the more modish phrase 'record players'. For the absence of such machines, Dexter tells us, the girls' elderly neighbours were 'eternally' – in the first instance in the manuscript – and then 'profoundly' grateful.

In her first appearance in the novel, 'the languid Sue' opens the door to Morse when he comes calling to interview Jennifer Coleby. Ascribing her initially the name 'Mary', perhaps even at this point, Dexter had not quite disentangled the three girls each from the other in his mind's eye. He excises this name and replaces it with Sue.

Invited to come in and wait for Miss Coleby, Morse however resists the invitation, Dexter originally writing:

'I think perhaps I'd better not'

And then:

'Do you think that would be wise?'

The question is expunged from the published novel. Given how events of the novel turn out, the answer would be 'no'.

The writer had originally described Sue Widdowson as 'a tall, pretty girl', qualifying tall by the phrase, written in black ink, 'fairly tall' before dropping any reference to her height altogether. The word 'pretty' is scored through twice, however, in favour of the bald adjective 'sad'. The reader could be forgiven for overlooking the significance of this word but it is an interesting choice.

Her sadness may reside in what seems to be a fairly unsatisfactory engagement to a metallurgist called David. Her dissatisfaction with her fiancé is symbolised in the resultant ingrained griminess of his hands. While he is what the manuscript version at any rate refers to as, 'the kindest man she had ever known', the weekend she has just spent with him which provokes her introspection 'all seemed so empty now'.

[The shops in Summertown have changed little in character over the years]

This vacancy only brings into sharper focus the selfishness she feels characterizes her desires. In lines again largely unpublished in the final version of the novel, Dexter writes:

'She remembered her mother telling her when she was just starting secondary school how selfish she was getting. She remembered one of her teachers – how vivid it still was in her mind! – telling her how selfish she was just the same. And she knew they had been right, and as she sat there in the kitchen, thinking of what to say to the kindest man she had ever known, she felt an overwhelming sense of loneliness and misery.'

Elsewhere, Dexter makes the blunt assertion 'Sue wondered at herself.'

'I'll write as soon as I get home,' Sue Widdowson promises her fiancé David as he sits in the 'deserted' carriage at Oxford railway station. This 'shouted' assurance is excised, however, and does not appear in the novel. She watches the 'rear light in the rear carriage gradually paling' in the gathering darkness.

The statement that 'The buses were dreadful on Sundays' is ruled through, however, as is her exact destination. In the manuscript, Dexter tells us that the nurse got off at Squitchey Lane, which is situated just beyond the parade of shops in Summertown.

'Poor Morse' she reflects, remembering the jealousy she had created in him during their dancing engagement but the epithet is dropped for the published novel. In contrast, her fiancé is 'not the jealous sort' although when Sue arrives home to discover Morse talking to her fellow lodger, Mary, she is 'furiously' jealous herself.

It is her jealousy which, in the end, results in Morse – in perhaps the most powerful phrase of the novel but which, again, did not make the published version – concluding of a particular course of action he is compelled to make:
'It was the hardest thing in life he'd ever had to do.'

All of this is to come. In Morse's first, formal encounter with Staff Nurse Widdowson, Sue's actual name is dropped just as casually into the narrative at this point as she leaves the living room.

Significantly, in Morse's first encounter with her, Dexter calls the nurse Mary initially, a name he would later ascribe to the shadowy third member of the household. It is not that the girls' names are interchangeable, but clearly the writer is rehearsing various possibilities before settling on which of the girls was where and when on the night of the murder.

'Was anyone in when you got back?' Morse asks and Jennifer's reply needs some careful redrafting. Still apparently indecisive about names, Colin Dexter writes in the first instance:
'Yes. Mary was in I know, and I think Milly was too. Josephine went to see Judi Dench at the Playhouse; she didn't get back until eleven.'

'Mary' is revised to 'Sue' and 'Josephine' – a name that has hitherto not appeared at all – becomes Mary. In the published novel, Mary's alibi is established as having been to the cinema to see *The Day of the Jackal*. Her original alibi in the manuscript was that she had been to see Judi Dench perform at the Oxford Playhouse. This small circumstantial detail allows us to date with some confidence the writing of this section of the novel to 1973 for in that year, Judi Dench was indeed at the Oxford Playhouse. She played the part of Vilma in *The Wolf* by Ferenc Molnar.

Asked to confirm Jennifer's alibi, Sue 'wasn't able' to be more precise.

'I'd be worried if you could, thought Morse.'

This comment is excised from the manuscript but Morse is clearly of the opinion that if the girls were so sure of the details, their alibi is likely to have been manufactured, the girls ensuring beforehand that their version of events is thoroughly synchronised.

As though aware their alibi has been exploded, after the Chief Inspector has made his exit, one or another of the girls look through the lounge curtains at Morse, still sitting in his car.

[Summertown Library dates from 1960]

'Would that be Jennifer or Miss Dark Eyes? He had the feeling that it wasn't likely to be the ice cool Jennifer,' Morse thinks although these thoughts do not make the final version of the novel.

Outside Summertown Library, and dwelling still, perhaps, on the cool Miss Coleby's charms, neither does the atmospheric line:
'He stood staring vacantly at the road, lost in thought.'

Jennifer is ultimately usurped in the detective's affections by Sue Widdowson, however, their next encounter accidental in every sense of the word.

Attending the hospital to exchange the crutches he has been given following a fall and the resultant sprain to his right foot while decorating, Morse stares at the floor and finds 'he could best while the time away by looking at the nurse's (sic) legs go by.'

One particular pair attracts his attention. 'Almost involuntarily' Dexter writes initially Morse 'decided' he would like to see the rest of the delicious 'child'.

'She was a honey' is the expression Dexter uses originally to describe the nurse. Dexter's sense of fashion is also rendered more precisely as he says that a nurse's uniform did more for a girl 'than all the fine feathers in Miss Selfridges.'

Morse says 'I'd love to have a talk with you again' but the nurse reminds him she is on duty.

'So am I, I suppose' is the detective's rejoinder in the manuscript.

Attempting to meet her after work, he interprets her reluctance as 'You've got a date'.

'I've got a date,' she confirms in the manuscript but this is amended in the published novel to 'Well, let's say I'm busy'.

The next day is no more successful a proposition. Dexter writes:
'Morse wondered mournfully if he needed to … if a … mournfully if his journey through the remainder of the week days was anything but a dismal formality.'

Morse tries to 'recover some of his lost dignity' when the nurse suggests a date on Wednesday evening.

Morse decides he had better not pick her up and, rather ironically, in view of the case he is investigating, wonders whether she could get a bus to meet him. When Sue says she is not a child, Dexter writes:

'Morse thought he ought not to add his comment to that.'

The line is excised in black ballpoint, however.

[The Randolph Hotel's iron porch dating from 1889]

He decides to ring Sue Widdowson with whom he has a date. In reflecting on alternative venues for their assignation, it is interesting that Dexter retains in the manuscript the real name of the most famous hotel in Oxford: The Randolph. The hotel is mentioned numerous times throughout the paragraph, but in the published version, the name is changed to The Sheridan.

When Jennifer Coleby answers the telephone, Morse tries to disguise his voice. Dexter writes this originally as:

'Morse tried in some inchoate way to speak like Morse didn't speak.'

But this is amended in black biro to 'as if he wasn't Morse'.

Initially, he asks to 'talk' to Sue but Dexter amends this to 'speak'. His contention that he is an old school friend is originally followed by the phrase 'said Morse gaily' before this is changed to 'replied the unMorselike voice.'

When Jennifer relays this introduction to Sue, Dexter writes 'Morse would dearly' but this is ruled through and we shall never know. One imagines Morse would dearly like to have been an old school friend, perhaps.

'Morse plumped for Morse' Dexter writes originally when the Chief Inspector is deciding how to refer to himself on the telephone.

'Morse wondered why he'd never learned to tell the truth', Dexter writes over his untruth about the double dinner date tickets he claims to have in his possession. He finishes the conversation in the manuscript version with 'Looking forward to seeing you'.

'The phone went dead' Dexter tells us originally though this line is excised in the published version. So, too, is his final benediction '... before Morse could wish her sweet dreams or any such endearing adieu'.

Morse's forgetfulness about his own inability to dance is expressed originally in stronger tones in the manuscript:

'He could no more ask the fair Miss Widdowson to dance than ask a pig to fly'.

The comparison is less than complimentary and perhaps this is why the writer excises the thought.

Dexter writes, originally, that Morse's 'long and deep' sleep the night before his date with Sue had been untroubled because 'his conscience must be clear.' The thought is ruled through in black ink, however.

'Since his accident', Dexter writes in the first instance – although this adverbial phrase is excised – Morse had been wearing a plimsol (sic) on his 'wounded' foot but now he wants to get back to 'somewhere near' normal. Morse, Dexter tells us 'could hardly believe that Miss Widdowson would be overjoyed to be escorted to her table at the Randolph …' but the sentence is overhauled heavily.

The original name of the hotel to which Morse squires Sue Widdowson is still in place in the manuscript and indeed its location 'in Beaumont Street' which is excised from the published novel. The Chief Inspector thinks that the management must keep 'a red carpet rolled away somewhere … Not that it had been rolled out tonight for Morse. In fact he had been unable to find any parking space in the hotel's restricted yard and was forced to park half way down St. Giles'.'

Having 'left' her coat, Sue 'walked with a light grace towards him, her long purple dress gently affirming the slimness of her graceful body.' He was aware of the strange and subtle promise of her perfume 'upon him.'

The Evans Room, to which Morse accompanies Sue, is originally described as 'set out with subdued taste and well-polished decorum' in which a small 'orchestra' (amended to 'band') plays some languorous melody top which a young couple dance 'oblivious to all else'.

Morse decides, originally, not to 'do too much' though this amended to 'give to his imagination too much free a reign'.

As the waiter arrives with the menu, Morse 'was glad to have welcomed the mild diversion'.

'What do we get?' was the way Dexter first phrased Sue's question. This is amended to 'Do they throw in the wine?'

'Morse looked up,' Dexter first writes here but then it is excised.

The writer begins to describe Sue's teeth as 'the firm' … but the adjective is dropped. As couples dance on the floor, Dexter writes, originally:
    'Morse watched Sue as she was watching them.'

But this detail does not make the published version.

'Morse told her about his car' in the first attempt in the manuscript but perhaps because the Chief Inspector leaving his car at the hotel so they can drink champagne has already been a topic of conversation, this becomes, simply, 'chattered as amiably and interestingly as he could and Sue was beginning to seem pleasantly relaxed … and Morse poured them/out for each of them/further another glass of champagne. The orchestra/band stopped'.

A houseman at the Radcliffe, Dr. Eyres, accompanied by a young woman, Sandra, who in the manuscript Dexter describes as 'about twenty' manages to inveigle Sue away from the Inspector with an invitation to dance. Morse is left to regale his 'decorating' accident to Sandra.

The whole episode leaves Morse feeling 'sick of a jealous dread'. Those same heightened feelings, characteristic of the tentative and awkward overtures which occur in the early stages of a romance are evinced later in the novel. 'As they reached the front door' Dexter writes, Morse asks Mary if she would fetch Sue down. Dexter phrases the question he asks the nurse originally as:

'Silly, I know, Sue. But I just wondered which room you slept in.'

In the published version, Morse does not confess to the foolishness of the question.

As their hands meet in what Dexter describes, first, as 'a natural accidental way' – revising this for 'accidentally beautiful' – Morse confesses his reasons for the question: 'If I come/I suppose if I come along past your house I'd like to know which was you' but the sentence is scored through with a line of green ink.

'She couldn't bear it' Dexter writes and turned – in the manuscript version – 'towards the house'.

It is, however, what Dexter originally describes as 'Coleridge's beautiful lines' from *Rime of the Ancient Mariner*, which Morse recalls here:

The bride hath paced into the hall
Red as a rose is she.

Morse turns his eyes away from the 'smouching' (sic) couples.

When Morse invites Sandra to dance, however, he rapidly realizes the 'extent of his own over-confidence'. His embarrassment 'that only the merciful ending of the music saved' Dexter writes before deleting the phrase is perhaps only compounded by what the writer describes first as 'gales' then 'a loud burst of laughter' when Sandra is reunited at their table with Sue and Dr. Eyres.

At least, in the manuscript version, Morse finds that the 'dinner is good'.

Sue's question 'Why did you ask me out, inspector?' is described firstly as 'a minor bombshell to Morse' and then as 'a bolt from the blue' before the writer settles on the phrase 'a big surprise'. Dexter needs to reword the description of

Sue. The published version appears encircled in the margin in black ballpoint, an arrow drawn to those lines Dexter has first fashioned then crossed through. His first attempt runs:

'Morse looked at her, the lightly coloured hair drawn back from her face/ back from her forehead, the freshness and delight of her young attractive face, her cheeks now lightly flushed with wine ...
He put his elbows on the table, rested his chin on his clasped hands and looked into those magic eyes.'

As they walk through what Dexter originally calls the 'swinging' doors of the hotel, in the manuscript he writes 'As they sat together, Sue put her arm in Morse's and he ...' but the thought is never completed, the lines excised. Instead, Sue talks of Jennifer and tells him '... you wanted to ask someone who knew her about her boyfriends and that sort of thing'.

There are four extra lines of prose at this point, which Dexter has ruled through:

'He had meant to ask her so many things, and he had been on the verge, as she spoke, of asking that one vital question about Jennifer that he must/that had to be put to someone very soon. But he could discover the answer ...'

When Morse's kisses her, however, he feels her body 'harden' in the manuscript version; 'she sat back in her seat'.

Sue's voice becomes, in the manuscript 'suddenly' matter-of-fact. Morse listens to the 'shaking' sobs as Sue confesses that she is engaged to be married. The windows of the car are 'steamed' and as Morse wipes away the moisture with the back of his hand, Dexter gives us the first biographical detail of the enigmatic Chief Inspector's past: he was an undergraduate at St. John's College twenty years earlier. In the published version, Dexter writes that 'life had somehow passed him by' but this final version is superscribed above the original expression, which is the more Larkinesque '... life seemed to have passed him by.'

The appearance of Jennifer Coleby at the door seems to wrong foot the author in describing Sue Widdowson's reaction. He makes several attempts.

'She opened the near side window and Morse ...' is excised in favour of 'She wound the window down'. In turn, this is revised to 'She opened the near-side door window and sounded as cheerful as she could'. Dexter attempts to interpolate this last phrase again after Sue has said, 'We don't want to get stopped for drinking and driving, you know' before finally settling for 'She wound the window down'.

A desultory conversation about the virtues of the Fiat car follows, reaching its nadir in Morse's prosaic observation 'Good after sales service' which does not

87

make the final, published version. Dexter employs the name Barclay's for the local car dealership but this is amended in black ink to Barkers which Morse has always found 'Pretty good myself'.

Upon being invited in for coffee, Morse says in the manuscript 'I don't think I ought, Sue'.

There follows a scene which was to become a commonplace of the television adaptations: a solitary Morse reflecting ruefully over a drink the turn his life has taken and, perhaps, the larger silence beyond it. Morse thinks of the first time he saw Sue 'as she opened the …' but the line is deleted, although it was 'Miss Dark eyes' who had indeed opened the door to him the first time Morse visited Jennifer Coleby at home.

Dexter quotes what he calls, originally, the saddest line 'in the whole of English poetry' but this is amended in black ink to the saddest line of poetry 'he had ever read' from *Thoughts of Phena* by Thomas Hardy:

> '*Not a line of her writing have I, not a thread of her hair*'

Morse stops at The Black Horse for a drink, but the name is amended to the White Horse for the published version. Since Dexter has so scrupulously altered all the names of all the real hostelries and hotels – The Mitre, The Randolph – it seems this has been adopted as a generic name for a public house, rather than suggesting the real White Horse in Broad Street, Oxford which is some way from Kidlington, Morse's location as he downs a double whisky. He thinks of Dr. Eyres and his own 'dark-eyed' companion – in the manuscript – 'with not' a hint of envy and then retires home, where, as he approaches the front door – he can hear his telephone ringing.

'Where was that bloody key?' Morse asks comically in the manuscript though the line is excised in green ink and does not make the published version. Nevertheless, he is defeated in being able to answer the telephone before it stops ringing. Thinking it may be Sue Widdowson, Morse implores the phone to ring again but it rings no more that night.

Of the desultory exchanges finally left to them, Colin Dexter wrote originally in the manuscript:

> 'For Sue, it was better than ten thousand goodbyes.'

Following Morse's final consultation with regard to his injured foot and as the Chief Inspector moves to bring the case to a conclusion, the detective dissolves almost into the crowds busy in the centre of Oxford. It seems an appropriate image with which to conclude our examination of the final draft of the novel which brought Inspector Morse into the world. The original version of the scene reads:

'It was almost two o'clock as Morse walked down from the Radcliffe Infirmary to the broad tree-lined avenue of St. Giles'. He thought of postponing his next task; but it had to be done sometime, and he was on the spot now anyway. His activities over the next hour would have seemed extremely puzzling to any attentive observer. Keeping to the right hand side of St. Giles' as he walked down towards ... he made his way towards the Martyrs' Memorial, Morse stopped at the first snack bar he came to, the Wimpy restaurant just opposite St. John's. He entered and spoke quietly to the small swarthy Italian tossing beef burgers on a heated griddle. Two waitresses were called into the discussion, there was a general shaking of heads and pointing, and Morse left. A few yards lower down the St. Giles' he stopped and entered the Bird and Baby, where he ordered a pint of bitter and engaged in earnest, quiet conversation for some minutes with the barman who turned out to be the landlord too. He was always behind the bar at lunchtime. It was all very interesting but to the vital question he could but shake his head. Thus Morse made his way. It was a long dispiriting business, but it was one that only he himself could do. He walked through the dozen likely places in the Cornmarket below the ABC Cinema, crossed the road at Carfax and started up the other side.

It was 3.45. Morse went over to the table in the corner and sat with his back to/facing the wall. He knew that the case was nearly over now, but he felt no elation. His feet ached, especially the right one. He was badly in need of something to cheer him up but he felt far from hopeful that anything was going to turn up. Again he took out the picture of Sue from his wallet and looked at the face of the girl he could have loved so dearly.'